CONTROLLED BURN

Stories of Prison, Crime, and Men

SCOTT WOLVEN

SCRIBNER

New York   London   Toronto   Sydney

SCRIBNER
1230 Avenue of the Americas
New York, NY 10020

Copyright © 2005 by Scott Wolven

Excerpt from *Bloodletters and Badmen*, copyright © 1973 by Jay Robert Nash.
Reprinted by the permission of the publisher, M. Evans & Company, New York.

SCRIBNER and design are trademarks of
Macmillan Library Reference USA, Inc., used under license
by Simon & Schuster, the publisher of this work.

For information about special discounts for bulk purchases,
please contact Simon & Schuster Special Sales:
1-800-456-6798 or business@simonandschuster.com

Designed by Kyoko Watanabe
Text set in Garamond 3

Manufactured in the United States of America

1   3   5   7   9   10   8   6   4   2

Library of Congress Cataloging-in-Publication Data

Wolven, Scott, 1965–
Controlled burn : stories of prison, crime, and men / Scott Wolven.
p. cm.
1. Men—Fiction. 2. Violence—Fiction. 3. Criminals—Fiction.
4. Prisoners—Fiction. 5. United States—Social life and customs—Fiction.
I. Title.
PS3623.O595C66 2005
813'.6—dc22
2004058310

ISBN: 978-0-7432-6012-1

For my grandmother and grandfather,
DLW and DWW

What the majority calls almost fantastic and exceptional for me sometimes constitutes the very essence of the real.

—Fyodor Dostoevsky, preface to *Demons*

Contents

I

THE NORTHEAST KINGDOM

The world is unstable, like a house on fire. This is not a place where you stay long. The murderous haunt of impermanence comes upon you in a flash, no matter whether you are rich or poor, young or old.

—Thomas Cleary, *The Five Houses of Zen*

Taciturnity

Robert, his son Bobby, and Ida sat in wrought-iron lawn chairs around the picnic table on Ida's back patio, drinking lemonade in the shade. Somewhere close, a screen door smacked against its wood casing. A car started. Parents yelled children's names up to heaven.

Harvest Lane ran straight for a mile off the main road, houses on both sides, and ended in front of Ida's brick and wood colonial, the last house on the left. Beyond the house lay a field and a sparse pine woods. Across the lane the field had been cleared into a building lot. Next door to Ida's house sat a newly built raised ranch with an inground swimming pool. Three massive oaks stood at the edge of Ida's property, between her house and the raised ranch. The trees towered over the back of her house, her neighbor's pool, and most of his lot. Robert's two-ton log truck rested in Ida's driveway.

"Lemonade is good, Ida." Robert spoke loudly. Ida was thin, with white hair and thick glasses helping her gray eyes. She looked down at her watch, and then over at Robert.

"Thank you, Robert. I don't get anyone stopping here much anymore." The shade from the big trees covered the patio. Ida kept on. "Years ago, I made lemonade for your grandfather when he delivered wood to us. Two cord, as I remember. He probably used that same glass you have now. A nice man, your grandfather," she finished.

Robert nodded. The glass was a thimble in his workhorse hands. His beard, black flecked with gray, needed a trim. Now he, too, looked at his watch. The bright sun sucked the morning dew off Ida's green crew-cut lawn, as the ancient sprinkler fought back with a wet rainbow. A false summer morning shower.

Ida patted her forehead with a red kerchief. "I made a glass for your father, too, when he delivered our wood. Some folks didn't like him, but he always treated my family well. Of course, he was a drunk. I never understood how he could drink so much and still work. I always saw his truck parked outside The Blue Flame."

Robert turned and spit in the grass. "He was a hard-working drunk." He had a heavy brow over narrow, blue eyes. He glanced at Bobby.

Bobby sipped his lemonade and looked at the trees. Just beyond them, he could see the neighbor's pool, and he could faintly hear the pool filter running. Bobby was clean-shaven,

but otherwise he and Robert wore the same face, minted in
different years.

A man walked across the lawn from the pool. He was
large, with a gut and dark, wavy hair. He wore a Hawaiian
print shirt, shorts, and sandals. He stopped at the edge of the
patio.

"Mrs. Stone," he called. "I—"

"Mr. Caporuzzi, this is Robert Maynard and his son
Bobby," Ida cut him off.

Caporuzzi ignored them. "Mrs. Stone, you can't be serious about cutting those trees down."

Ida blinked behind her glasses. "Oh, I'm not going to cut
them down. I'm much too old to do my own cutting. That's
why I hired Robert." She nodded at Robert.

"Mrs. Stone, those trees have been there a long time."

She turned toward her house, an old two-story farmhouse
with a brick façade and a full porch on the front. "This concrete patio is new, twenty-five years ago, but the rest of this
house is mostly patched together from what was here before
Christ was Christian. Who are you to tell me about how long
trees have been on my property?"

"Don't be this way," Caporuzzi said. "I just meant that
the trees have historical value."

"You're right. My grandfather was born here in eighteen
fifty, and he wrote about those trees in his journal. Every day
he'd record what the weather was and some days, he'd make
a note about the farm or the land. Those trees appear in several of his entries." Ida took a sip of her lemonade. "Wait
right here. I'll show you." She stood and walked into her
house, the screen door closing behind her with a smack. The
sky was brilliant blue with one perfect white cloud, drifting.

Ida emerged from the house, and the screen door smacked again as she sat back in her lawn chair. She held a crumbling, leather-covered notebook. She adjusted her glasses, and started to read coldly.

"This is dated July eighteen ninety. It says, 'Today I went into town, and walking back up the hill, I saw my oaks. They stand out over the other trees.'" Ida gently flipped forward several pages. "'Doctor Hatcher came down from Hanover today to help with the baby, but he was no help. We lost a little girl. I stood out under the oaks and looked up at them. They've grown so much since I first noticed them. The middle one seems smaller. Maybe they're a mother, father, and child.'" Ida sipped her lemonade.

Caporuzzi shook his head and put his hands on his hips. "Why are you cutting them?"

Ida shrugged. "No reason, really." She turned a thin wrist so she could see her watch.

"I could call the selectman and file a complaint."

Ida nodded. "I did call the selectman, eight o'clock this morning. Old Vern Hafner. I think I woke him up. He said, Hello, and I said, Vern, this is Ida Stone. What's town ordinance say about running a chain saw on a Saturday morning? And he said, Ida, you can do anything you want after ten o'clock. Just wait till ten. Then he hung up."

Caporuzzi checked his watch. It was nine fifty-five. He shook his head and glared at Ida. "I'm going downtown to file a complaint with Hafner. He'll enter it into the town board minutes and we'll get an injunction from the town justice."

Ida nodded again. "Well, you might do that, except today's the day that Vern goes over to the VA to get treatment for his paralysis. I forgot to tell you he mentioned that to me on the phone. And since Vern is the head of the select-men, no one else can enter items into the board's minutes." She noted her watch. Robert sucked air through his teeth. Ida turned to Bobby and smiled.

Caporuzzi's voice had an edge. "Mrs. Stone, do you know what I do for a living?"

"Well, some rumor's gone around that you sell encyclopedias, but I don't pay much attention. I've never heard a vacuum running from your place, so I assume you aren't a Stanley Steemer man. People who sell vacuums always have the cleanest homes, my mother used to say. I mean, do you work? I didn't even know you were employed." She sat staring at Caporuzzi.

"I'm a special investigator with the Vermont State Police."

"You must be especially good at finding things, then. I'm sure you'll find some more shade for your pool." She took her glasses off and began cleaning them with the red kerchief. She cleared her throat and spoke very softly. "My grandson Raymond used to play under those trees, right here, in the shade." She put her glasses back on.

Caporuzzi shifted his feet. "Mrs. Stone, I'm sorry your grandson is in prison. But he was a drug dealer." He nodded. "Your grandson sold drugs."

"Not that you know of. The police set him up with an informant who was already on parole and Raymond bought some marijuana from that man and that's all of it. He told me."

"He was doing more than that, Mrs. Stone."

"If he was doing more than that, how come you didn't catch him at it?"

"We already had all we needed. The state's attorney was satisfied."

Ida's eyes were dark. "And what was wrong with walking across the lawn some evening and introducing yourself and saying to me that the boy I raised practically since he was born was in with the wrong crowd, that I should talk to him? If I had known, if you had told me, don't you think I'd have talked to him? My own grandson?"

"It doesn't work like that," Caporuzzi said softly.

"Well, this doesn't work at all. How do you think I'm ever going to see him again? I couldn't afford a decent lawyer for him, I don't drive anymore, and he says on visiting days I'd have to sit across from him at a table that's bolted to the floor, in a room full of other people with guards around. I couldn't take it."

"I'm sorry."

"How long were you going to live next to me before you decided to come over and tell me that you arrested him?" A car door slammed and a neighborhood dog barked.

Caporuzzi shook his head. "The law doesn't compel me to tell you."

"I got a letter from him yesterday stamped Northeast Regional Correctional Facility. He has to shower with other men, he told me. He's going to be locked up for three years. Thirty-six months." She took a deep breath. "I won't be around in thirty-six months." She pointed at Bobby and then Robert and then the trees. "Those trees are coming down." She looked straight at Caporuzzi. "I don't know where you're from, but don't think you can come up here and set my house on fire to stay warm in yours."

"Mrs. Stone, I was just doing my job."

"So were the Romans." She shook her head. "As my father used to say, you're a bird even if you never flew."

"Don't do it, Mrs. Stone. Don't cut those trees."

"Officer Caporuzzi, you're not married to that woman who flops around your pool in her underwear, so those two little boys of yours are bastards. I'm not in the habit of providing shade for bastards." She stood up and looked at her watch, then at Robert. "It's ten o'clock. Cut those trees."

Caporuzzi made a stop motion with his hands. "Mrs. Stone, you shouldn't do this."

"Cut 'em."

Bobby went out to the truck, opened the cab, and put on his climbing belt and spikes. He pushed a red earplug into each ear, then checked the oil and gas in the limb saw. He decided to start on the tree closest to Harvest Lane and work his way back. The butt of the first tree was huge, at least ten feet around. He dug his spikes in and started to climb.

When he reached the top, Bobby could see for miles. There was his father's woodlot, with red and black trucks sitting around idle on a Saturday. The high school looked tiny, the cornfields of Percy's farm a green-and-yellow carpet to the river. The mountains seemed close. It was as far as he'd ever seen in his whole life. Bobby pulled the chain saw's cord and the saw roared. Carefully cutting in the pattern of a reverse spiral staircase, just like his father had taught him, Bobby rained limbs and branches on the ground far below. The noise of the saw deafened him even through the plugs, and the limbs fell silently. He could see the patio. Mr. Caporuzzi was gesturing, pointing at the trees and Mrs. Stone, all a silent film because of the saw. Caporuzzi walked back across the lawn, past his swimming pool, and disappeared into his house.

Bobby worked through the morning, and by noon there were only three naked trunks standing, the ground completely covered with tall piles of cut branches. Ida sat on the back patio in the blazing sun, watching. She held the leather-bound notebook tight to her chest. Bobby went to the truck and pulled out the big saw. He put the three-foot bar and chain on it, checked the gas and oil, applied a file to the chain's teeth. He lugged the big saw back to Robert, who stood waiting by the butt of the first trunk. Robert took the saw in his hands and jerked the starter. The saw roared, louder than an airplane.

Robert back-notched the trunk and scored the front of it with the saw. He moved around the tree and drove the chain blade in deep, cutting straight toward his back notch. Bobby watched closely. Sweat poured off Robert's forehead, sawdust stuck in his beard. Then he was through.

He lifted the saw out of the cut and shut it down. In the silence, the top of the tree was moving, faster, now faster toward the ground.

Robert looked over at the sun-filled patio. Ida was gone.

She walked into the house through the kitchen and up the stairs to the back bedroom. She sat on the bed. This was where Raymond slept when he came to visit. The bed was neatly made, with a light white quilt for summer and two pillows. The trees were gone now, as she looked out the side window, and for the first time, she had a different view. She saw the pool and the house. One of the little boys had on a bathing suit and was headed out the back door.

Her phone started to ring downstairs. She sat on the bed and listened to it ring several more times, then stop. She stood and walked to the hallway, gently shutting the door to

Raymond's room and crying as she did. The phone started ringing again, but she didn't intend to answer. She didn't like talking to people while she was crying. Ida sat at the top of the stairs and wiped her eyes with a tissue and then blew her nose, faint drops of blood too fine for her to see escaping, driven by an invisible pressure, measuring and remeasuring her time.

Outside Work Detail

Early that morning, the storm moved south over the dark Quebec woods, crossed into Vermont at Lake Memphremagog, the inland sea of the Northeast Kingdom, and made the shore at Newport, rattling windows in trailers and shacks, shoving woodsmoke back down their rusted stovepipes. The thunder tore through the trees, then hit the bare farm fields around Saint Johnsbury. The air inside my cell shifted from the sudden pressure, carrying the boom, and moved something deep in my chest. I woke. I lay there on the top bunk, listening to the thunder muffled by the thick concrete. My cell mate was a man named Don Wilcox. He sat on the stainless steel toilet bowl that was attached to the wall directly at the head of his bottom bunk. He was smoking a cigarette, flicking ash into the toilet between his legs.

"Coop, you up?" he asked.

"Yeah," I said. The cell was dark except for the red ember of his cigarette, moving in an arc when he flicked it.

"Some storm," he said. "Must be something, if we can hear it in here."

I nodded in the darkness. "Sounds bad," I agreed.

"I hope it doesn't scare my kids," he said. Don Wilcox was in his late thirties and had a wife and three young boys in Greenville, Vermont, about twenty miles away. They always came to Saint Johnsbury on visiting day. Wilcox had been convicted of arson. He'd burned an outbuilding on his mother's old farm in an attempt to get some insurance money after his mother died. He'd been in trouble before, years back, and the prosecution held his prior record against him. He was just beginning to serve his ten-year sentence. For the past eight months, he'd been my cell mate, my ninth in a little over sixty months at Saint J prison. I could barely see him in the dark, only the red eye of his cigarette.

"Your kids scared of thunder?" I asked.

"My middle boy is," he said. "Makes him wet the bed." The stubble on his chin raked the collar of his work shirt. "I used to yell at him when he wet the bed." He was very quiet, and I heard the thunder. "I wish I was out."

There was nothing to say to that. He talked for a while longer, stories about his kids I'd already heard, about how he hoped his wife was faithful. I drifted off, back to sleep. When I woke up again the cell was filled with cigarette smoke. I heard the voices of other inmates in the cellblock, heading to lunch. I swung myself down to the concrete floor from the bunk and went to eat.

I stepped off the chow line carrying a lunch tray and found a seat alone, at the end of a long stainless steel table. The mess hall was full of other prisoners—sometimes Saint J holds over a thousand men, although it was built for eight hundred—all wearing street clothes, jeans and flannel shirts, because the Vermont Department of Corrections never got around to installing proper heat in any of its facilities. Winters were too cold for the customary prisoner jumpsuit, and the Vermont winter could last till May. Even beyond. The storm had stopped, and now the noise was just the usual loud voices cursing, laughing in a nasty way. As I ate my sandwich, an old con came and sat across from me. I looked up at him.

"You Ray Cooper?" he asked. His beard was a mess—gray, black, uneven—and he was almost bald. He wore a green work shirt. His lungs sounded bad. I recognized him as a trusty from being in the library, but I couldn't think of his name. A faded jailhouse tattoo, the letters FTW, were inked on the back of his left hand.

I nodded. "Yeah," I said. "So what?"

"You're bein' transferred," he whispered. The mess hall made it hard to hear him, with all the voices bouncing off the walls and ceiling. He looked around at the other prisoners and the guards by the door and leaned closer. He did it so easy. Anyone looking at him would have thought he was adjusting the seat of his pants. "I heard them say Cooper this morning, they're just waiting for the paperwork." He lowered his voice to less than a whisper, barely moving his lips, not looking at me. "Don't tell anyone, they'll stab you in the night." He smiled as another prisoner walked past looking for a seat. He breathed through his smile, through his missing teeth. "They're jealous. But you've got to try to live."

I looked at the dim sunlight coming through the windows set thirty feet above the floor and covered with screens of heavy-gauge wire. Thick, black dust covered the screens. I had just turned twenty-eight and had eighteen months to go on my eighty-four-month sentence. "When are you out?" I asked.

The old man stood, his back crooked, and held on to the table with one hand. "When I say hi to Jesus, that's when I'm out."

He shuffled away, toward the chow line and the other prisoners. He was gone when I looked up again. Vanished into the crowd. Left me to think about The Farm, the minimum-security prison run in Windsor, Vermont, by the Department of Corrections. Two hundred men were held at The Farm. There aren't many prisons in the Vermont system—two in the north, higher security Saint Albans or Saint A, as inmates called it, along with Saint J. The sex offenders were housed in Newport, and there were facilities at Rutland and Woodstock, each holding a mixed population of convicts. If prisoners managed to avoid fights and develop clean records of good time, they usually ended their terms at The Farm, which had an extensive wood shop and sawmill operation, all located on seven hundred acres of fields and surrounding hills. Only the fences and concrete cellblock buildings set it apart from the Vermont landscape. A day at The Farm counted as two and a half regular days in the bizarre math of good-time calculations, because everyone was a low-security risk and expected to go to work and go to programs. There were GED classes, anger management, AA meetings. All things that normal people did outside the fence every single day, without expecting good time in return.

That night in the cell, Wilcox was sick from bad chow. I watched him hard from then on, harder than before, but he never gave any indication he knew I was leaving. Ten years stretched out in front of him and filled whatever part of his mind wasn't devoted to his boys. Sometimes I doubt that he even knew I was in the cell with him.

The paperwork came at the end of July, and they transferred me south in an unmarked, four-door Jeep on the last Friday of the month. I didn't say a word the whole ride down out of the Northeast Kingdom—just sat cuffed on the rear seat, sweating from the sun. Watching the trees and country and what I could see of the sky pass by the shatterproof windows. We pulled up to the entrance guardhouse at dinnertime, but I was held in the sergeant's office for in-processing, shackled and cuffed to a steel ring welded to a metal desk.

It was humid and hot that August, with hundred-degree days coming one on top of another. Every night I stood at the window of my new cell and watched heat lightning flash over the fields and high fences of the facility. The Farm itself was surrounded by a five-foot-high barbed wire fence, topped with razor wire. The short fence was old, a reminder of a less violent time. A dirt road ran around the outbuildings and prison dormitory, allowing the guards to ride patrols between the outside, shorter fence and the new inner, electrified fence. The inner fence was twenty feet high, crowned with two strands of razor wire. The last six feet of the fence were angled inward, making it difficult to climb from the inside, and the razor wire was set at such a pitch that scaling it from the outside required a professional level of skill and tools that no average person would ever possess. Full voltage ran through the fence wire, and the hum filled the facility, as if an angry swarm of bees was floating in the woods, waiting.

I wasn't an innocent man. When I was seventeen, I was set up by an informant during a pot buy. I did three years and got out. A year later, I smashed a truck window one night near Essex Junction, Vermont, and took a large briefcase I saw resting on the front passenger's seat. I was drunk, not that drunkenness makes such things okay. I opened the case with an acetylene torch and they took me into custody three hours later, but for those three hours, I was in control of the contents of that briefcase, which happened to belong to an investigator for the Vermont State Police, who kept four pistols locked and loaded inside, along with some of his police identification. He wasn't on assignment that night. Parked on a back road, he was visiting his girlfriend, which was bad because he had a wife and his girlfriend had a husband. So he wasn't where he should have been and this hit the local paper and the paper in Burlington and made the state's attorney eager to put me away for causing so many problems for a law enforcement officer. I got the maximum time allowed on the illegal hand-gun possession, all four guns, all felonies, plus theft, breaking and entering, destruction of private property, and illegal possession of official identification, which is another felony. The list seemed to grow longer each time I appeared in court, as my public defender struggled to remember my name, once asking the judge for a continuance on behalf of his client Mark Copper and appearing surprised when his honor spoke from the bench and asked him who that was, as I sat next to him in shackles and cuffs whispering *Cooper, Ray Cooper*. My name didn't matter anymore, at that point. I was sentenced a month later, credited with the time I'd already served but bound over to serve more, my priors held against me. I stood for the maximum fall, eighty-four months.

The parole board consistently denied me parole, and after three hearings I wasn't considered again, since I was termed "close to maximum release date." The board put in the special transfer order that sent me to The Farm to serve out my time, to free up my cell in the fiercely overcrowded system.

The trooper, who remained on the force, took an active role in keeping me locked up, attending all of my parole hearings, relating the story of the guns and the pain of his divorce and the terrible part I played in it. Every time, after he had his say, he stood up in his full dress grays with medals, adjusted his Sam Browne belt, and put his black Smokey-the-Bear trooper hat over his honest crew cut. He gave a sharp nod to the old Vermonters who made up the parole board as he marched out of the room, back to his job, back to towns and situations that needed his bright justice, something I had tarnished.

I doubt the old Vermonters even saw a human when they turned back to look at me, and certainly, after the first couple of years, I began to feel less and less like someone who'd once lived down the road from them and got drunk and did something stupid. I felt like what their eyes said I was, someone who needed to be in a tiny concrete room behind high fences and armed guards and locked down but good, for as long as the locks held and longer if possible. It was probably only procedure that I was transferred to The Farm, nothing more. In their hearts, no one on that parole board wanted me one step closer to the door—one step closer to being in a grocery store in their town, one step closer to walking down Main Street.

I answered the questions they asked of me, that I planned to go live with my sister Elizabeth in Essex when I was released, and I produced an old letter from her, giving me permission to live at her house and inviting the parole board to call her if they had any questions. She had stopped visiting me after three years, and I didn't blame her. She still wrote occasionally—wrote when my grandmother died—and I was still planning on living at Elizabeth's house when this was over and that was all I could ask of anybody.

My girlfriend at the time of my arrest, Mary, used to come see me. When I first got in and Mary would arrive on visiting day, I always talked to myself in my cell, to make sure prison hadn't worked its way into my voice. *Hello, Mary,* I would say, *thanks so much for coming.* Mary had stopped visiting me after eight months. For a long time, I kept the last letter from her, explaining why she wasn't going to visit anymore, folded in a notebook. "Dear Ray," it began, "I have some hard things to say and I hope you know how difficult this is." I understood. People have lives. My sister wrote that she'd read in the paper about Mary's wedding, four years after I'd been inside. Good for Mary. Now I was at The Farm and there was an end in sight.

Fall came, and the leaves colored and died. The ground froze solid and the first of the snow came. I went to some programs and the library, but with the snow I stopped. I sat up all night watching it fall under the halogen lights that made it seem as if the sun had descended to Earth at midnight. I felt no interest in programs anymore, they weren't helping me. My days counted two and a half whether I attended or not, and I actually began to think that I might get out, and about what I would do then.

Two weeks before Christmas, a corrections officer named Walter approached me as I got on the morning chow line. Would I like an outside work detail, he asked. I said okay, since it was probably the only time I'd get out until after Christmas and I wanted to see if I could handle it outside. I went back to my cell after chow and put on my old army field jacket with Riley stitched above the left breast pocket—I always wondered who Riley was and what he'd done, to have his name stitched on the jacket and then to have it find its way to the prison laundry lost and found.

I walked to the guards' station desk, next to the outside door. Walter stood there with a guard named Frankie, who sat behind the desk, and they filled out the paperwork on me, signed me out of the facility, and popped the electronic lock on the door, sending me into the open yard and the early morning snow.

Another inmate, Russ Harper, was already outside, smoking a cigarette. I recognized him from the library and around. He was a programmer, the first one in his seat at AA, kept the best journal in anger management. He wore a green field jacket with an attached hood pulled up against the snow and small patches of West German flags on each shoulder. We started to walk through the snow toward the back field, following a set of tire tracks. Russ offered me a cigarette.

"No thanks," I said. The snow was coming heavier now.

The facility got smaller as we walked away, one thin line of smoke coming out of a pipe on the metal roof, the screen of snow drifting down in front of the halogen lights.

"Haven't seen you much lately," he said.

"I stopped programming," I said. "Couldn't see the point." We were walking side by side on the tire tracks.

"You got denied?" he asked. It was a fair question.

"Yeah," I hedged. "I've been denied three times and I didn't think programming here was helping. I thought it was hurting. Besides, the board won't see me again."

Russ nodded, his red hair poking out from under his hood. "I understand," he said. "To each his own." He had moved off the tire track and was having trouble walking through the crusted snow that held powder underneath. He stepped back on the tire track. "My mother died after I'd been in for two years, so I understand things. My father's dying now." The hood covered his face. "Cancer."

"That's too bad," I said. "I was at Saint J when my grandmother died." We walked along next to each other. "What's this work detail about?" I asked.

"Walt didn't tell you?" he said.

"No."

"Well, it's no fun," he said. A fast snap from the electric fence made him turn around, but there was nothing to see and the fence returned to its hum.

We stayed directly in the tire tracks to reach the top of a small hill that rose along the back field. Beyond it lay another long, snow-covered field, and in the rear right corner sat a blue Department of Corrections pickup truck. We started to walk down to it. The truck was parked about fifty yards from the electrified fence. Behind the truck stood

another separate, fenced-in area. Square, about fifty by fifty.
Cables ran out of the back of the truck into the small fenced-
in area, where a generator was going. We walked down the
hill, and the facility disappeared behind us. We stumbled a
little in the snow, trying to stay in the tire tracks. For the
first time, I felt the cold biting my face. I could see my
breath. The hum of the electrified fence was constant. The
ground angled slightly to the fence, then there was the
guard road, the low fence, and the woods. I realized the area
inside the small square fence was the prison cemetery.

Reb Phillips sat on the open tailgate of the truck, smoking a joint. He made no move to share it with us. The army
field jacket he wore bulged at the arms and around his thick
chest. A black ski cap came down around his ears. He
laughed as we came up. Reb was the outside trusty and most
of the guards were scared of whatever racket he ran.

"Look what they send me," he said. "An old-time programmer and the new boy." He shook his head.

In the back of the truck lay two large, black body bags.
Reb motioned at them. "They came down two days ago, but
with the snow and all . . ." He stuck his thumb at the sky.
The snow was falling steadily and the clouds showed no
break. "Usually, we bring the Turbo Cat back and do it that
way, but the one Cat's broken and Town of Windsor got the
other for snow removal." A gated section of the chain-link
fence hung open, and two ground warmers, like little jet
engines, were stationed five feet apart from each other, the
bare ground turning to mud beneath them. The tops of
white wood crosses poked up through the snow crust.

"How do you end up here?" I asked.

Reb motioned at the graves. "Vermont law, if your people

can't or won't pay to have you carted when you die anywhere in the state system, they send you here." He grinned. "And I plant you." He pointed again in the direction of the graves and pulled two shovels out of the back of the truck. He smacked the end of the body bag on the left. "Dig this one first, he's from Saint A, he was a good shit. This other one"—he nudged the body bag with the shovel blade—"he's from Saint J and fuck him, I heard he was an old rat. We'll bury him at three feet instead of six, so he can feel that ground freeze and thaw for the rest of forever."

"How'd you know he was a rat?" I asked.

Reb gave me a hard stare. "Was he a friend of yours?"

"I don't know," I said. Russ was already digging the first hole.

Reb grabbed the body bag and yanked it out of the truck, letting it fall onto the snow. He reached down and pulled the zipper back, and I heard the big metal teeth separate. The dead con's eyes were closed, and he had a mass of gray hair swirled around his head. Snowflakes landed on his cheek and stayed. Reb stood there, waiting for me to answer.

"I don't know him," I said.

"Then shut the fuck up and dig." Reb looked over at Russ digging. I started to dig too. Reb climbed into the bed of the truck and shoved the other body bag to the ground. He opened the zipper on that one, and I could see the dead man's head, his closed eyes. There was a smell. "That's one thing you don't get on the outside, to watch your own grave dug," Reb said. He walked to the front of the truck, leaving Russ and me digging. The smell of the joint drifted faintly in the air. After a while, a pickup truck drove down the guard road and stopped opposite us, between the fences. We all stood up straight, and then the truck continued on, marking us on the head-count sheet for that shift.

We had just finished putting six feet of dirt back on the first man, along with a white cross, when Reb came over and pointed at the woods and whispered. "Look."

At the edge of the woods, barely visible through the snow, a tiny herd of deer, including a large buck, moved to the tree line near the low, outside fence.

"I count five," I said softly. The wind was blowing from the woods, so the deer probably didn't smell or hear us.

"Me too," Reb said. "Five. That's a good size buck."

We watched as the deer pawed at the snow and shifted positions. Then the buck took two quick steps and jumped the low fence, landing on the Jeep track between the two fences. He stuck his head to the ground and came up chewing, with a noseful of snow.

"Must be grass or apples or something over there," Russ said.

"Wild apples," Reb said. He pointed at a tree that hung over the two fences. "I think that's an old wild apple tree. The truck breaks the crust on the snow, and then the deer can get at them." Two other deer quickly jumped the low fence and began pawing around on the guard road. It was hard to see what they were coming up with. The snow was falling steady, and I could barely see through one fence, let alone two and beyond. The chain link is twisted into the shapes of empty diamonds, and looking through two makes everything take on a dark zigzag pattern that shifts, the shadow of something that was never there.

I waited and my eyes settled directly on the next deer, a doe. She took three steps up to the fence and got into the air.

For some reason, though, she didn't get high enough, just landed directly on the wire and stuck there. A terrible noise came out of her mouth.

"Jesus," Russ said. The young deer struggled and became more entangled in the concertina wire. I watched her shake violently, only to have the wire shake back and stick deep, just below the ribs. The other deer took off down the guard road, hopping the fence with white tails showing for a second, gone into the snow and woods. "Reb, call a C.O.," Russ directed. There was a radio in the pickup truck.

"I'm not calling anyone." Reb shook his head quick. He looked at the wire. The deer hissed and made a short, high-pitched scream. "That wire will fuck you up every time," he observed.

Russ put his shovel down. "I've got to take a leak." Slowly, he walked around the ground warmers and out of the fenced cemetery. He walked until he was about ten feet away from the electrified fence, directly in front of the impaled deer.

"Those other deer are gone." Reb shrugged. "Just like people." He spit into the snow.

I couldn't see Russ clearly through the snow and the one fence, but I knew he wasn't taking a leak. From the back, it looked as if he was crying.

Reb picked up on this. "Hey program boy!" he yelled over at Russ. "Can't take a deer stuck on the wire, how are you going to settle accounts on the outside?" Russ was crying out loud, and now we could hear him. Reb must have hated that sound. It set him off. "What the fuck makes you think you'll ever get out, you long time bastard? I've seen your sheet, you still got fifteen years to do! I'll be fucking planting you back here! Nobody's going to pay to have your sorry ass buried in Vermont, you worthless fucker!"

Reb went and sat in the truck. I heard Russ whimpering. The deer was quiet now except for a terrible rasping every time she tried to breathe.

Reb tossed a beer can in the snow. He got out and hefted the ground warmers into the back of the truck. I was digging the second hole. Reb handed me a white wooden cross that was hand carved. He showed me the bottom, with the word RAT burned into the wood.

"Put that shit on top of him when he's planted," he said. "I'm heading back. Bring your shovel and lover boy and lock the gate when you come." He got into the truck and drove across the field and over the bank. I could still hear Russ. The deer was dead. The electronic fence made the same low-grade hum. I bent to dig, and when I looked up, Russ was gone. I couldn't see his tracks, because the snow was coming down too hard. The deer's head was pointed down at the snow, and underneath her, I could just make out a spot of bright red, spreading into the white. The deer's eyes were wide open and all white too, as if the snow was somehow inside her. White was the only color except for the gray of the chain-link fence, the shiny razor wire, and the green of my jacket, close to my face. All the rest was snow.

I was determined to give the man his full depth, but I couldn't do it. At about three feet, I ran smack into several large rocks, none of which I could move with my shovel. I wasn't going to walk back to the facility and try to get a pry bar that I probably wouldn't be allowed to have anyway. I tried again with the shovel, but I thought the handle might shatter and I stopped. I grabbed the body bag and dragged

it over the snow and dropped it in the hole. I covered it with
dirt and put the cross on top. Then I locked the cemetery
gate, put the shovel over my shoulder, and walked back to
the facility. The snow was coming down so hard that when I
looked back over the field I couldn't make out the individ-
ual graves, or my own tracks coming out.

I checked back in, and Phil, the guard on duty said,
"Where's Harper?"

"I don't know," I said.

"Did he walk away from work detail?"

"When I looked up, Inmate Harper was gone," I said. I
told Phil about the deer, but I don't think he listened. Later
I heard that Russ Harper had been given a disciplinary hearing and six months was taken off his good time for walking
away from the outside work detail. I never heard anything
else about it, whether cancer took his father or not. I'm sure
that after he walked away from work detail, they wouldn't
let him attend the funeral, not even in shackles.

I watched out my cell window, the spring and its mud season
and the rain. I tried to stay away from the other prisoners as
much as possible. I heard the occasional scuffle at night.
Noises that came and went in the dark. I'd been hearing
them ever since I got in, almost eighty-four months earlier.
My days were counting, all at two and a half, moving faster.
Soon I'd be done.

Late on a Thursday afternoon, I was called to the main
administrative offices by a sergeant. He took me in to see the
chief officer, Rogers. We just got your paperwork, and your
max release date comes up on Sunday, he said. Since we don't

release anyone on the weekend, that moves your release up to eight a.m., tomorrow morning. We'll have an officer from the field supervision unit in White River Junction give you a ride to the station in White River. So be ready to go in the morning.

And that was it. I was terrified and didn't come out of my cell for the rest of the day. I didn't even try to place a call to my sister. I didn't want anyone to know. I didn't want to be stabbed. Late that night, pacing, three steps then turn, three steps, turn, I noticed the letters FTW scratched into a concrete block near the cement floor. The marks looked old, probably made years ago by some con who was in for good. Fuck the world.

The guards came and got me at seven the next morning and I was awake, hadn't slept all night. I was standing there, had my property inventoried and stuffed it all in a gym bag that had been with me for the whole bid. The guards took me up to the fence and walked me to the main guardhouse at the front entrance and told me to wait there. An unmarked four-door Jeep pulled up, and the gate snapped its electronic lock. I stepped out and went to sit in the front seat.

"Get in the back," the officer said. "State regulations."

I sat in the back with my gym bag. We started on the road to White River Junction.

"You probably won't make it," he said, "most of them don't. Just don't come back here, because we'll hit you with the max all over again. Don't go stealing any guns, you freak. Keep your hands off stuff that isn't yours. And he's still on the force, so remember it's a small state. Personally, if I was you, I'd move. Florida, lots of construction work down there since the hurricane and plenty of sunshine. You can still work, can't you? Nothing happened to you, right? Nothing happened to you on the inside that will keep you from working, did it? Frankly, I don't know if people up here will even give you a job. So think about it, it might be a trip worth taking. Don't harass anyone at the station, I'm telling the Amtrak employees who you are and what you were in for, so no funny stuff. Just go up to Essex. Don't bother any of these people."

By the time we got to White River Junction, the sky was dark. It was just beginning to rain as I walked up the concrete steps to the Amtrak station.

I stood there in the waiting room with my DOC-issued rail ticket. For the first time in my life, all the people around me knew I'd been to prison and that I'd never have that stench off of me. I remembered the deer and how she maimed herself by struggling. I stood still. I became part of the wall. I didn't move or blink or breathe. Nothing. All I heard was the thumping of my own blood, running everywhere at once. Sweat started running down my forehead. When the train came, I forced myself to walk across the concrete platform and find a seat alone. I was soaked, with rain dripping off me. I kept touching my gym bag, as if it held something important. It was soaked, too. I opened the zipper a little. My clothes and papers were as wet as I was. I thought about the man I'd buried shallow. For a minute, I was him, his dead face wet from the rain seeping through the canvas body bag. When I looked up, the rain was coming down even harder.

On the train the conductor came by in a uniform and asked for my ticket and I already had it out. He said, "Where are you going?" and I tried to say Essex Junction, but my voice cracked badly on the first syllable and it just came out like a high-pitched squeak. He laughed at me. "Essex Junction," he said, "I think you meant to say Essex Junction. Work on your voice there, mister." He went down the line, taking tickets and talking.

I put my hand over my mouth, like I was resting it there, thoughtful, and started to practice it, right there on the train. I spoke quietly into my hand. *Hello,* I said, *it's nice to see you.* I couldn't bear the thought of my voice cracking in my first words to my sister Elizabeth, so I cleared my throat and continued softly under my hand. *Hello,* I said, *it's wonderful to see you.*

El Rey

Before the logging operation in Maine closed, Bill drove a big rig and generally got paid more than I did. I ran a saw. I drank quite a bit. It ate into my wallet. We kicked around in Maine. In a bar outside Houlton I managed to sneak a right hand in and knocked a guy out for two hundred dollars. I thought I was a boxer.

We finally ended up at Bill's mother's house in Saint Johnsbury, Vermont. On the way there, we stopped at a reservation and picked up some tax-free cigarettes for her. She didn't seem happy or sad to see us when we pulled up. She didn't hug Bill, but she did take the cigarettes. "Are these for Mother's Day?" she asked Bill when he gave her the cigarettes. "They are now," he said. "You don't have to pay me for them." Hard times had made that love, for the two of them.

In the morning, I walked down to Thompson's woodlot and fifteen minutes later, I was working. When I first started in late May, my back took a month to get into shape. I hurt so bad some nights after work that I slept on the hardwood floor. My hands hummed from running the chain saw all day. My spine rusted tight. I didn't think I'd be able to raise myself out of a bed to walk to work in the morning.

Bill started to cash a check, driving a log truck down from Quebec for a big outfit, and then the accident got him, crushed him against the steering wheel. He sat totally paralyzed in a wheelchair at the house. He could look out the window and see me at the woodlot, and I would wave up to him, give him the high sign. Nurses from the county came in to feed him. His mother made sure the door was open so people could get in. A buddy of his, Tom Kennedy, came to see him once in a while. Bill's voice still worked, and I imagine he gave those county people hell for the hour they were there. He hated being paralyzed. Beyond hate, really.

I ran the chain saw most days, filling firewood orders as they came in and trying to stay ahead, as people got ready for winter. We had as many as fifteen orders a day, mixed cords and half cords. Gary worked with me, a wiry little local with a mustache and a tattoo on his arm that said AMBER inside a hand-drawn heart. Gary ran the hydraulic splitter and packed the cut cords into the rusted dump truck. He was a good worker. We managed eight cords a day, ten if nobody drank heavy the night before. The heat would drive it out of you anyway, sending you behind the shed to puke before eleven o'clock in the morning. We all did it, kicked sawdust over it, and kept right on working. The log trucks made the turn off the road down into the main yard and the French-Canadian drivers would hop up into their cherry pickers and unload themselves right onto the big stacks, and then walk over to the pay shed where Harold sat, answering the phone and paying cash for any decent load of logs that happened to come his way. He didn't care where the logs came from or whose property they were. The log business can depend a lot on timing. You leave a load on the ground in the forest too long and bugs can get at the wood and ruin things quick. Or maybe somebody crossed a property line on a clear-cut and had to get rid of some wood fast. Once the wood found its way into Harold's yard, it was his, and the exchange rate being what it was, the French-Canadians made sure plenty of wood always showed up. Bill watched all day from his bedroom, and we'd talk about my day at the woodlot when I got home.

"Better than television," he said. I always knew if Tom had stopped by because Bill would be drunk. Tom left beer and sometimes whole bottles for Bill. "He keeps me in the juice," Bill said. Then I'd join him for a drink in his room and look out the window at the woodlot where I worked all day.

Whether it was the heat or the work or the booze, I don't know, but the job made everybody pretty mean. In the beginning of August, somebody made a comment at lunch about Gary's pregnant girlfriend and the next day Gary came in and took a swing at a new guy who was standing near the barn and came back to work the splitter with a bloody nose and the beginnings of a black eye. About two weeks later, a log truck

pulled in and unloaded and while the driver walked across the
yard, I looked at him through my goggles for a minute with
the chain saw still running. He gave me the middle finger as
he walked into the shed and I started to move fast. I shut the
saw down and took off my Kevlar chaps, headphones, plugs,
and helmet, tossed my goggles into the sawdust and met him
as he came out the shed door. I hit him right in the face and
then again and he fell to one knee, and I picked up an ax handle that was leaning against the shed and started beating him
on the shoulders and ribs and back. I hit him so hard that the
ax handle stung my hand to the bone. As he lay in the sawdust, I reached into his right front pocket and took the money
he'd just earned from the log delivery. Somebody helped him
back to his truck and he sat there for a while and then drove
out. Later that night, I counted five hundred dollars with my
hurt right hand and then I went out and walked to the corner Gas Mart and treated myself to a twenty-four-pack of cold
beer. I drank three of them before I made it back to my sweltering attic room at Bill Doyle's house. Bill was howling,
laughing upstairs when I came in.

"You gave it to that frog," he called down to me.

I walked upstairs. The door to Bill's mother's room was
closed with light coming from underneath. I poked my head
into his room. Bill's face always looked tight and wind-
burned, from all those years driving a truck. "That's what I
feel like doing, every day. Jumping out of this fucking chair
and giving it to somebody."

"I hurt my hand doing it," I said.

"You've got another one, don't worry about it," he said. "I
wish Tom could have seen that."

"Tell him about it," I said. Bill talked about Tom Kennedy

so much, I felt like a big deal to be mentioned in the same company.

"I will," Bill said. "He loves a good fight."

The next day I came home from work and called up into the house from the bottom of the stairs like I always did, and there was no answer. I went up to Bill's room and opened the door and got sick. Bill really wasn't there anymore, he'd sprayed most of his head onto the wall with a shotgun blast. A faint blue haze hung close to the ceiling. The wheelchair was there with the headless torso slumped in it and the shotgun on the floor. A bunch of beer bottles and a liquor bottle, cheap whiskey. Empty. For so much violence in such a small room, you'd have expected to hear noise, an echo, something. But it was silent. His mom left after the funeral, went to Florida to live with her sister, and I moved out too, got a new room in another house.

In the last week of August, two shiny black four-by-fours with tinted windows and New York plates pulled off the highway and down into the main yard. I assumed they were new homeowners, maybe up from New York City, looking to fill a wood order for winter or with some land they wanted clear. I was wrong.

The man who got out of the first truck was a dapper-looking Hispanic, with the whole outfit on. The sunglasses, the gold chains. Shirt open a couple buttons. The creased black dress pants, black pointy shoes. He spoke with a thick accent. Harold, his gut hanging out of his denim coveralls, walked

out of the pay shack and shook hands with the Hispanic man.
The rest of us stopped working, wandered over and listened.

"Hello," he said to us. "I am Melvin Martinez, and we are
looking for strong men to spar with." His accent was so
thick I could barely understand him. Several more Hispanic
men got out of the trucks. Young, muscular, with black hair,
all in blue warm-up suits.

Harold looked over at the men standing by the trucks.
"Where'd you last fight, up in Quebec?"

"Yes," said Melvin. "We started in a logging camp up
there and are working our way back down to New York City."
He pointed at one young man wearing red boxing trunks.
"That is El Rey," he said. "We're preparing him for the pros."

"Did he win?" asked Harold. He took a red kerchief out
of his back pocket and wiped the sweat off his forehead and
neck.

"El Rey has not lost," Melvin said. The gold chains around
his neck caught the sun. He wore a thick gold bracelet on his
left wrist, along with a gold watch and some rings.

Harold considered this a minute. "What weight class are
you looking for?" he said.

"El Rey will fight anyone, he doesn't care, as long as there
are gloves and a ring and timed rounds. No headgear. No
kicking. Regular boxing."

Harold nodded and his beard moved. "Well, usually
before a fight, there's another match, there's more than one
fight on the card. Got anybody else who wants to fight?"

"Yes," Melvin said. He turned to the men who had come
out of the trucks. "Hector will fight. He is El Rey's sparring
partner." One of the men raised his hand and began to take
off his warm-up jacket.

"Fine," Harold said. "That's fine. We'll get something going here, just give me a minute." He turned around and pointed at Gary. "Take a sledge and a tape and some of those long iron stakes by the shed and make me a ring here." Harold turned to Melvin. "How big do you want?"

"Twenty feet is good," Melvin said. "We've got gloves with us, sixteen ounces, for better protection. Do you need them?"

"Yeah," Harold said. "I don't have any boxing gloves sitting around."

Gary held a stake as I pounded the top of it with a sledgehammer. The sawdust jumped around the base as it went into the ground. We used the tape to measure out twenty feet for the next stake, and snapped a plumb line to make sure the thing was square. The blue chalk dust hung in the hot air after the line drew taut. We drove in all four stakes and tied a white rope all the way around.

Harold and Melvin held a private conference on the hood of the closest four-by-four, and then Harold came back over to us. Everybody was standing near the pay shack, looking at the ring. Harold ran a hand through his hair and spoke as he walked toward us.

"I put two hundred fifty dollars on it, so let's see what happens," he said. "If you want to bet, go give it to him." He pointed at Melvin. "No odds, just straight win by time or knockout." A couple guys walked over and gave Melvin some money, but I wanted to wait.

Harold turned to George Hack. George was a big man, a drinker and a bar brawler. He generally ran the skidder if we were in the woods, and he always worked the big saws on any cutting job. He played football for Saint J high school and still talked frequently about it although it was years ago, and

I'd seen him knock the daylights out of Jimmy Conrad, the bouncer over at Suedon's Bar on Main Street. We prepped the ring area with a rake while George went into the shed and came out without a shirt on, just a pair of jeans, his work boots, and the sixteen-ounce boxing gloves on his hands. Some of his flab hung over his jeans. Hector was smaller than George, but there was no fat there. Hector had on boxing trunks and shoes laced up to his knees. His gloves. Melvin agreed to take the first round as referee. He wore a white towel around his neck.

The bell rang and both men came out of their corners toward the middle of the sawdust ring. George took a wild swing that hit nothing. He almost slipped. He was already sweating. Hector set him up fast. Two quick left-handed jabs, one to the face, one to the body, and all the time, the right fist was waiting, held back, the pressure building, as George's hands chased Hector's up then down, still back, the bombsight zeroed in on George's left ear, then boom! Right on George's ear, clean and solid, and George's knees buckled and his head bounced when it hit the sawdust. George wasn't even conscious yet tears were coming out of his eyes. Two guys jumped into the ring and pulled George into the back of a pickup truck. As they turned him over, sawdust stuck to his chest and his face and his crotch, which was soaked. He'd wet himself from the shot to the head.

Harold suddenly pulled me off to one side, behind the pay shack. "Go get me Tom Kennedy," he said in a low voice. He handed me a hundred-dollar bill. "Tell him there's more to go with that."

"Let me fight El Rey," I said.

Harold shook his head. "I want to win," he said. "You

can't take an ax handle out there in the ring with you." He talked out of the side of his mouth and then turned toward me. "Besides"—he looked straight at me—"you don't have the life in front of you that Tom does."

I took the money and walked along the stream that made the back border of the woodlot. It brought me out at the end of Langmore Street and Kennedy lived one over, on Hartsel Avenue. I walked down the cracked sidewalk, full of frost heaves.

Tom Kennedy was Harold's main tree climber for any residential job that went up over a hundred feet. At least, that's what everyone at the woodlot said, but I'd only seen him there once. I'd heard more about him through Bill than anything else. In reality, Tom Kennedy collected weekly pay from Harold just for staying away from the woodlot. His temper and drinking were two of the things I first heard about when I came to Saint J. Tom Kennedy was also a local fighting legend. The last I'd seen him at the woodlot, he'd yelled at Harold like I'd never heard anybody do, ever. You could tell he was a mean drunk just from the force of his words. Told Harold to suck it, then stood there and waited for Harold to say something. Harold didn't say anything. I was nervous, going to get Tom Kennedy.

He sat on the wood porch of his big house, drinking a beer. Bill told me Tom's father had been the first Irish cop to leave Boston and tried to bring something to the force here in Saint Johnsbury. Tom had tried to be a cop too, for a little while, but something went wrong and after a short time, he simply wasn't a cop anymore. He didn't wear the uniform and he didn't drive the car anymore, he just faded out of that life into another.

There were kids running around, some his, some his girl-friend's. Some belonged to other people and I thought that ten years from now, those same kids wouldn't even hang out with anyone named Kennedy. I walked up the sidewalk to the bottom step of the porch.

"Hi, Tom," I said.

"Hi yourself," he said. "What does Harold need done?" He tilted his head back and drained his beer, tossing the can on the porch. His reddish hair looked bronze in the sun.

I took the hundred-dollar bill out of my pocket and handed it to him. "There are some men from New York City over at the woodlot, looking to fight." I indicated the money. "Harold says there's more after that."

"What kind of men?" he asked. "Niggers?"

"No," I said. "Hispanic men. From New York City."

Tom made a noise I took as a laugh. "They aren't from here," he said. "They're not local. There's no Spanish Ver-monters." He looked at me. "How tough are they?" He touched his own cheek. "Some black guys got hard faces, their faces can break your hands. And they take people's crap all the time, so they can get pretty mean. Hispanic guys aren't like that."

"The one guy just sent George Hack to the hospital," I said. "Hurt bad."

"George Hack?" he said. "George Hack couldn't fight my sister."

"Well, he went down pretty hard," I said. I thought of the tears coming out of Hack's eyes, how he'd pissed himself.

"Did you think George Hack was tough?" he asked. He started lacing up his work boots.

"Maybe," I allowed.

"George Hack was a fat slob," Tom said. "I should go over to the hospital and beat him in his bed just for losing so bad." He pushed on his right ear with the flat of his hand and I heard the cartilage crack. "He couldn't box," he said.

"He got hurt," I said.

"How big is this guy I'm fighting?" he asked.

"Big," I said. "Probably two twenty, maybe more."

"You know what they say?" he asked.

"No, what's that?" I asked.

"It isn't the size of the dog in the fight, but the size of the fight in the dog," he said.

"Oh," I said. Tom stood and stretched his arms out. He sat again. "Thanks for looking in on Bill those days." I appreciated Tom buying Bill's booze.

"We went back a long way," Tom said. "Used to be good friends, he knew my father when my father was still alive. I made sure his mother got around in the snow sometimes." He waved it off. "Local friends, that's all." He pointed toward the woodlot. "Think I can beat him?" he asked.

I took a while to answer. "No," I said. "I don't think you can. If he's better than that guy who fought George Hack, no way."

"Is he mean?" Tom asked.

"I don't know," I said.

"Oh, you'd know," he said. "Heard you beat some frog with an ax handle a while back. Bill told me."

"Yeah," I said.

"You should learn to use your fists," he said. "Learn to box."

"I know how to box," I said.

He snorted. "I'd have shoved that ax handle so far up your ass you'd have coughed splinters," he said. "You want to see

boxing? Come watch me right now. I'll show you boxing."
He stood and stretched. He looked at one of the little kids
running in the street. "A plastic helmet and toy gun don't
make a soldier."

"You should've seen what this guy did to George Hack,"
I repeated.

"Did he piss his pants?" he asked.

"Yeah," I said. "How'd you know?"

"I been around," he said. He showed me his right hand.
There was a raised scar between his first and second knuck-
les on one finger. "I hit a man so hard his front tooth was
lodged in there." He pointed at the scar with his left hand.
"All the way to my bone," he said. "That's what happens
when you put that torque on your punches. I'm not just talking about a brawl. I'm talking about boxing, like my old
man taught me." We walked down the sidewalk in silence
and as we turned, I stole a glance at his right hand again.

We walked back the way I'd come and by the time we got
to the woodlot, there were probably fifty people crowding
around, looking at the little ring and staring at El Rey, who
sat on a stool in the corner with his back to the four-by-
fours. He and Hector were talking in Spanish, along with
Melvin.

Harold came over to us as soon as we walked onto the lot.
He went to shake hands with Tom, but Tom brushed him
away.

"Two hundred dollars besides what you already gave me,"
Tom said.

"Done," Harold said. He reached into his coveralls and

pulled out two damp hundred-dollar bills and gave them to Tom.

Tom stripped to a pair of shorts and sneakers, no shirt. On his back, along the right shoulder blade, he had a half-finished tattoo that looked like a shroud with a scythe and the words GRIM REAPER in shaky script. It was the color of mold. Tom got into the ring and sat in his corner. He looked over at El Rey.

Melvin and Harold both got into the ring and after they looked at each other, Melvin clapped his hands. Everyone was quiet.

"Ladies and gentlemen, this is going to be a twelve-round fight with two-minute rounds," he said. He pointed at El Rey. "And in this corner, wearing the red trunks, The Hispanic Panic, undefeated in his career, weighing two hundred and twenty-one pounds, The King of Knockout, from the Bronx, New York New York, El Rey!" The other Hispanic men whistled and clapped and El Rey stood up and shadowboxed for a minute, finished up with a flurry of short punches, then remained standing, dancing on his feet, loose. Melvin stepped out of the ring and Harold cleared his throat and pointed to Tom Kennedy.

"In this corner," he said, "weighing one hundred eighty-five pounds, The Pride of Saint J, Tom Kennedy!"

And when his name was called, Kennedy got off his stool and danced for a minute, bobbed and weaved and threw a few light punches and we all cheered him, really cheered him, and he remained standing too, moving and ready.

Harold motioned for both guys to touch gloves and they did and Melvin hit the bell. El Rey came out fast, moved up to Tom, swung and missed, and Tom made two quick jabs at his ribs and backed off, his hands held at an almost awkward angle, his feet always moving. They danced together and El Rey jabbed with his left, pulling his right hand back, jabbed again, and swung full with the right, but Tom wasn't there anymore, he moved back and to the side and then in again and bang! bang! two fast rights to El Rey's head and the bell rang.

Tom came over to the corner and sat on the stool and I gave him some water, which he spit into the sawdust. Melvin and Hector were in El Rey's corner, talking loud in Spanish.

Tom spit his white rubber mouth guard into his right glove and spoke. "Watch me now, and learn about those fists," he said. He popped his mouth guard back in and stared across at El Rey's corner. The bell rang and he stood and I grabbed the stool out of the ring.

He and El Rey met in the middle of the ring and El Rey juked left with his head, then right, swung, but Tom ducked under, and one two! shots to the body and one two! again, one to the solar plexus. I saw the look on El Rey's face, I knew it, and as he brought his hands down to cover himself, Tom slammed the right side of his head with the glove, hard, and again, and there was blood flying, and I thought for sure Tom would step back, but he stepped forward, closer, almost hitting down on his target and bang! a strong left hand to El Rey's nose and the bell rang.

Tom sat on the stool. He was breathing heavily, sweat all over his body, and we toweled him down and they were screaming in Spanish in the other corner. Tom popped his mouth guard out. He didn't say anything. He looked mad. He stared across at El Rey's corner and put his mouth guard back in. The bell rang and Tom came off the stool like a rocket. He threw a couple light punches and El Rey took a step back and Tom stepped up, closer again. Then he swung twice, fast, and it was like punching bullet holes in a paper target—El Rey didn't feel the shock until the punches were through him.

I didn't know exactly what happened next because Tom moved so fast and his back shielded me from seeing the punches directly. All I could watch were his shoulder blades, moving with each punch, over and over and all to the body of El Rey, and El Rey's face looking at me over Tom's shoulder, trying to stay alert, and now Tom was on El Rey's head, he found the range, it was a right, another right and a right, and El Rey fell to his knees hard and Tom kept hitting him, blood coming out of El Rey's ear onto the sawdust, and El Rey went down face-first, the sawdust jumping up as his head hit the ground, his eyes closed, and it was silent. The Hispanic men jumped in the ring and popped amyl nitrate capsules under El Rey's nose and he didn't move and Tom just sat there on the stool, with blood on his chest, as they picked El Rey up and carted him back to the trucks and presumably the hospital.

It stayed quiet as men collected their money from Melvin and came over to congratulate Tom. He was still sweating, still trying to catch his breath. A bruise was starting on his face from a punch I hadn't even seen. The marks on his chest seemed to glow red. Slowly, he took his gloves off with his teeth.

"You want some help?" I asked.

"No," he said. "I'm just taking my time." After a while he put a shirt on and he and Harold talked and then I watched him walk back the same way we'd come over, along the stream toward his house.

*   *   *

I have a different job now, handling shipping and packages
for a company near Montpelier. Every time I drive past
Thompson's woodlot and see the men working there, I'm
glad it's not me. Last night, I was up late—my wife had
taken off to see her mother, who was sick and lives just down
the block. I had a couple of beers and turned on ESPN. The
late-night fight card had El Rey on it. He looked bulked up.
I decided to walk to the corner store for some more beer and
snacks. It was mid-November and snowing pretty hard.

Tom Kennedy was at the store. He smelled. He was in the
back, looking at the coolers full of beer.

"Hey Tom Kennedy," I said. "The Pride of Saint J."

He turned and stared at me. Sometimes when people
drink a lot, they have a certain look about them, a fog they
have to get through before the world reaches them, and
Tom's gaze had retreated into that place. He didn't know
who I was.

"Hey, mister," he said. His jeans were ripped and he wore
an old flannel shirt.

"I've got El Rey on ESPN over at the house," I said.
"Want to come over and watch?"

"What?" Kennedy said.

"You know, El Rey," I said. "That guy you fought over at
Thompson's." His hearing seemed a little weak too.

"I haven't been in a fight," he said.

"No," I said. "Three years ago."

He looked at me. "Three years ago? What the hell's three
years ago got to do with today?"

The question hung there in the air. I had the luxury of

thinking about three years ago, or watching TV, or waiting for my wife to come home. "Nothing," I said. "Just thought you might be interested."

"I'm interested in getting some fucking beer, but that asshole won't sell it to me." He pointed at the high school kid behind the counter. "Says I'm already drunk. Right?" Tom Kennedy gave him a deadly stare.

"I'll call the cops if you don't leave the store," the kid said. "I've done it before on him," the kid continued. "He makes me." A phone hung on the wall behind him. Tom Kennedy headed back to the beer cooler. He grabbed a six-pack of bottles and ran out of the store, into the snow. I tossed a ten-dollar bill on the counter and ran after him. He was already headed down the sidewalk.

"Hey, Tom," I called. "Wait up."

He turned fast. His face seemed to come clear out of the snow and I knew that he remembered me.

"I shot him," he said. "He begged me to do it and if you had been a good friend to him, you'd have done it."

"What?" I said.

"I blew his head right off," he said. "What was the point of him living if he didn't want to live?"

"You mean Bill?" I said.

"That's right," Tom said. "But it should have been you. To pull the trigger."

He hit me in the side of the head with a full bottle of beer. I lay there in the snow and went in and out of it. I heard a police siren going through the night, a sound you don't hear very often in Saint Johnsbury, through the quiet streets and houses, echoing out into the huge forest of the Northeast Kingdom and beyond.

Crank

That morning, we all met at the blue diner on Route Three north of Jefferson, New Hampshire. Red Green, Converse, and me. Converse picked the meeting place. I'd driven past it plenty of times lately, hauling logs down from Quebec to the woodlot in Littleton.

Red Green was as high on crystal meth as I've ever seen anyone. He was shining. Up to that point in my life, I never used much meth. But I saw how much bikers around New Hampshire and Maine were willing to spend for big batches of the stuff and how high they got. Converse must have seen the money in it too.

Red Green slid in next to me and across from Converse. He'd driven for three days straight from San Diego to get there. He didn't order anything to eat. Red Green's face was thin, the type of face you get from too many cigarettes and drugs and not enough food, and his red hair was in a pony-tail. He wore a gray T-shirt and jeans. He looked around the diner, the booths made of plastic red leather and gold trim.

"This place is futureless," he said. "How can so many people live without being alive?" He glowed with ill health.

Converse nodded.

Red Green kept on. "I need a house with a barn in back for the lab," he said to Converse.

"Right," Converse said. He always looked ready to go from slow to fast in a hurry.

"I need food, guns, chemicals, a dog, and some supplies and a stove, a good stove, not some shit stove and then you say 'Fuckin' Red Green dicked me out of money,' hey forget that, I need a good stove, get me a good stove to begin with and we'll avoid those things in the future." Red Green was sweating, although everyone else had a sweatshirt or flannel on, even a coat. His T-shirt was wet.

"I'm way ahead of you," Converse said. He drank his cof-fee from the thick white cup.

"Well, I don't see it, is all, I don't see it," Red Green said. "All I see is a bunch of no necks eating bacon." He waved vaguely at the other men in the diner. "Where's the property, let's get this fucking show on the road."

"You're high," Converse observed.

"Fuck it," Red Green said. "If you're gonna bug out, then go do your bug thing—if not, pay me and let's roll. Live free or die, I see that all over, let's play that game."

"Have Ray drive and follow me," Converse said, and he nodded at me. "Leave your rig here," he said to Red Green.

"Finally," Red Green said. "Finally, finally, Jesus Christ thank the black rubber on my ass that this show is finally finally *finally* on the road." He stood up and we left the diner. Outside, the air was sharp. My breath came out in little ghosts. Converse walked across the parking lot, headed toward his own truck. He crossed in front of three loggers— I knew one guy—going into the diner, and they all gave him plenty of space and as much friendliness as their flat faces could come up with. Converse was a big man.

Red Green got into my rusty full-size Ford Bronco. He sat in the passenger's seat. He looked at himself in the side mirror.

"Jesus holy lord," he said. "Here I am and all I want to do is get business rolling and everyone is all against our former best friend and pal buddy from Sandy Eggo, the incomparable Mister Reddish Green." He looked at me.

"Converse is always like that," I said. "Don't take it personal." I was busy following Converse out of the parking lot. I drove around a couple of log trucks with their engines running, and a cement truck turning, keeping the load alive while the driver got his coffee.

"Well I make the best crank north and west of Philadelphia," he said. "That's not some bullshit you hear in a bar, like the rest of life's crap, like 'Oh, I love you,' or 'You're handsome,' or 'I like small tits,' or some horseshit. My fans are legion. I know for a fact that right this minute up in Belt Montana, there are bikers using my stuff and they are very happy sturdy stouthearted men engaged in the work of whatever god they happen to believe in."

"What the hell does Belt Montana have to do with any-thing?" I asked.

"When you move as fast as I do," he said, "the country is a very small place. Since the advent of the internal combus-tion engine, we've been able to zip around quite a little bit." He tore the plastic and foil top off a pack of cigarettes, popped one in his mouth and lit it with a silver Zippo. "The no smoking sign has been turned off," he said. "We're in New Hampshire and smoking in all areas is encouraged." He looked at the hole in the dashboard where the radio should have been. "No helmets up here," he said.

I followed Converse and turned off the county road, head-ing up into the Northeast Kingdom. The Connecticut River was on our left for a while, serving as the border into Ver-mont. We kept driving north.

"Converse should remember this," Red Green continued. A log truck passed us going south. "I have a skull in my head and it glows white hot."

"What does that mean?" I asked.

"It gets dark early in my part of the world," Red Green said. He looked out the window at the passing trees and mountains. "I'm no clown, thanks to the glorious death angel that imparted to me the ways of the sacred chemistry."

"I think you sampled too much of your own brew," I said. I turned right, following Converse wherever he was going. Now we were in the land of dirt roads that cut off with no signs, rusty dented mailboxes on posts, no names, old soaked papers inside from who knows when. Converse was driving a brand-new Ford Bronco.

"My life is none of your business," Red Green said. "I live in a world you never could, every day is a naked scissor fight." He started to laugh. "My veins scrape themselves," he said. "I'm self-cleaning." He laughed. "I'm the Red Green machine."

He kept on, a steady stream for an hour or more, until we reached the house and barn Converse had found for us in the deep woods, miles away from anything. We set up shop right away. When I first met Converse, he was married and had a kid. He ran a small logging business. I worked for him, running a chain saw one summer. He was a local, like me. I think his wife ended up in Florida with their boy, but I never asked him. Maybe she cheated on him. A girl cheated on me the summer I worked for him, so maybe I'm making unfair connections. All I know is that selling drugs seemed a lot less dangerous than running that saw every day. I made a lot more money with the drugs, too.

My job was to move the packages around. Most of the biker bars in New Hampshire and Maine signed on after a sample. I even had one guy in a bar outside Portland ask me if it was Red Green's stuff. People were staying up for months on the crystal I handed out. I took some of the crank myself, as much as I needed to complete deliveries. My blood caught fire as it kicked in. I was awake most of December, making runs from the barn in the deep snow. The guys that ran the plows bought from me and sent sparks off their blades as they smoked the icy roads.

At some point during the blizzard of January, I went into a bar on the New Hampshire–Maine border to have a few drinks. Doggie's Place. It was a cheap joint, filled mostly with loggers and bikers avoiding women or too ugly to get women. Talking about not working, engines, and debts. Who owed money around. Some guys played scratch-off

games for drinks. I sat at the bar and drank a beer and a shot
and another beer. I needed to come down a little.

"Hey," some guy called across the bar. "Hey, man, I know
you." He was a big guy, hair cut short, with tattoos on his
forearms. He was talking to me. He got off his stool and
walked behind me. "You sold my buddy some bad shit." He
put a big hand on my right shoulder. I shrugged it off. "My
buddy ended up in the hospital."

"I don't know you," I said. I turned on my stool to face
him. The inside of my head was pounding. I wore a knife in
a sheath attached to my boot and I wanted to knife him,
right in front of everybody.

"You're the dope man," he said, slobbering drunk. "I
know your tat, man." He pointed at the back of my right
hand. I have the Chinese symbol for strength tattooed there.
"I saw you in Portland, with the good stuff at Ed-Jack's Bar."

I put a ten on the bar and walked past him toward the
door. Outside it was dark and the snow was coming down in
white sheets. I didn't notice the cold. I made it over to my
Bronco and I'd opened the driver's side door when I realized
he'd followed me. He and a buddy were standing right
behind me.

"I told you I knew you," he said. "Don't run. We need to
talk about what a piece of shit you are."

I reached under the seat and came out swinging with the
tire iron. I laid it across his temple twice before he fell down
in the snow. I think I hit him again. Several times. His
buddy was edging back toward the neon of the bar.

"Do you want some?" I asked. My blood moved so fast I
thought it would burst through my skin.

"No, man," he said. He backed toward the bar door.

"You're damn right you don't."

"Stay away from me," he said. He went inside the bar. I climbed into the Bronco and went to put the tire iron back under my seat. There was blood on the end of it.

I backed out of the parking lot and took off. Past the snow-covered motorcycles and trucks and the guy still laying in the snow. I think I misjudged and ran over his arm. I didn't stop to look. I was sweating, fogging up the inside of the Bronco. All the way across New Hampshire, I wiped the inside of the windshield with a towel so I could see.

Every time I stopped at the lab to see Red Green, I did some crystal with him. His stuff was powerful. One night, after finishing off a supreme bag of crank, I headed for Boston. My intention was to go to a strip bar and end the night with one of the dancers. I never made it. I don't remember how the fight started, but I swung a baseball bat at a couple of high school kids in a snowy parking lot somewhere and drove off. I got turned around and ended up passing the halogen lights and razor wire of the big penitentiary above Nashua.

"Hello my brothers in arms," I screamed into the dark and snow. "Fuck the world!" I wanted to ram the truck right through the fence. I'm surprised I didn't.

In the spring, Converse hired a lookout named Wayne. I met Wayne once on my way out of the barn after picking up a new batch of stuff from Red Green. Wayne was standing by my Bronco wearing tiger-stripe fatigues and a black jungle cap. He had a large pistol in a holster around his waist.

"I'm Wayne," he said. He didn't hold out his hand or anything. "Don't let anyone follow you up here."

"I don't," I said. "I'm careful."

"Be carefuller," he said. "You look like an asshole." Then he walked into the woods.

I got into the truck and left. But I think Red Green heard him, and probably Converse heard him, if Converse was sitting in the house then. So Wayne and I would have to have a talk and straighten things out at some point. It stayed on my mind all day. It boiled.

By the time I got back to the barn I was coming down from some crystal I'd taken two days earlier and stumbled in on Red Green. I'd spent the whole day in my truck, hating Wayne. I took some new stuff, the last of a bag I had, to keep me fresh.

"Hey," I said. "I'm going to kick Wayne's ass, want to watch?"

Red Green was in the middle of messing with a blue flame under a glass tube. He looked up at me. "What are you going to do, kick his ass up around his ears? Make him eat dirt? Hold on a minute, I'm coming." He glanced around the lab and then came outside with me.

"Where is he?" I asked, sweating.

"He has a perch in a tree way up on the hill." Red Green pointed off into the woods. "Come on, I'll show you." He started to walk quickly through the woods. "Are you going to make him call you Daddy?"

"I might," I said. Now that I was thinking about it, I got a little nervous. Wayne had a gun and I didn't. Red Green was smashing through the woods and talking at the same time. We were covering ground fast.

"Wayne looks pretty tough to me," Red Green said. "He might smack you around like a girl."

"Thanks," I said. We trekked toward the hill. I was dodging limbs.

"Hey Wayne, old friend," Red Green called ahead. "Ray's going to scramble your eggs."

"Come on," I said.

"Ray's going to introduce you to the truth about being a man," Red Green said.

We came to a clearing on top of the small hill. From the trees above, Wayne had a perfect view, probably as far off as three miles. He kept an eye on the operation from up there.

"Hey Wayne," Red Green shouted up into the trees.

"What?" It was Wayne's voice coming down through the trees.

"Ray's here and he wants to kick your teeth in," Red Green said.

"I'm coming down," Wayne said.

We heard some movement in the trees above us and then spotted Wayne. He was still wearing camo and was belted into the tree with climbing gear.

"Just a minute," Wayne said. I watched his hand move over the climbing clips. He was going to rappel out of the tree.

For a second, he was suspended, about seventy feet above the ground. Then he moved a little, down, then dropped like a stone, with the ground rushing up hard to meet him, and as he bounced on his face, I heard the dry crack of two shots. He lay there on the forest floor, not moving. Red Green went over to him.

"Jesus," Red Green said. "His gun went off. Friendly fire."

Wayne was bleeding, and he just lay there, not moving at all.

"Is he dead?" I asked.

"As far as I'm concerned," Red Green said. "I'm not in the business of saving lives." He knelt next to Wayne and felt his neck and wrist for a pulse. "The Great Spirit has a new member of the flock," he said, standing.

Converse was coming up the path behind Red Green. "Fuck," I heard Converse say. "Ray," he said to me, "get the hell out of here for a minute. Give us some space." I walked back down the hill and stood by my truck. I paced around. I kicked the tires.

Red Green and Converse came out of the woods. Converse went into the house. Red Green came over next to me.

"This is a tough break," he said. "It calls for the octane." I followed him behind the house, to the barn lab. "Look at it this way," he said. "Everyone should get to die twice. In Chinese, there are many ways to say death and one of them implies, Hey, you've just finished what you were saying. I think Wayne, in his humble way, was done talking." He opened the door. The whole place smelled faintly of gasoline. He snorted some powder and began prepping a set of works for his arm. He started to move around the lab, talking to me. He lit a cigarette.

"You look like the devil just raped you," he said. "Wayne, who gives a fuck about Wayne? We'll burn this place with him in it. He'll get the blame. The newspapers can say Wayne did it, and everyone's happy."

"Is Converse pissed?" I asked.

"What am I, therapist to the stars?" Red Green said. "You fucked around a little and it cost. At least Wayne didn't shoot you. He aborted himself."

"He would have shot me," I said. "He was reaching for his gun. That's why it went off."

"You're mental," Red Green said. "I can't be party to your mental illness." He ran the needle into a vein on his left arm and fired himself up. I watched him begin to blaze. "Johnny Rockets," Red Green finished.

"You saw him," I said. "The gun went off, he must have been reaching for it."

"That's what cops typically say," Red Green said. "The suspect is suspected of shooting hisself." He started to laugh.

I nodded.

"Let me tell you a crazy story," Red Green said.

"Okay," I nodded.

"A couple years back I decide to give up the drug shit. I mean, that's it, no more, I'm Mister Clean and Sober. So off I go, globe-trotting. I'm doing a Zen thing. I had saved decent money at that point." He took a swallow out of a beer can and held it out to me. I shook him off and he kept on.

"I end up in Peru. And by some nasty joke of the god-king, I get taken prisoner by the Shining Path."

"You must have been fucked," I said.

"Fucked would have been good at that point," Red Green said. "First they shot these two German tourists that were with me. Left the bodies next to the railroad track, then dynamited the railroad. I was blindfolded, in a cell, and no one knew I was there. After torturing me with a rubber hose and a riot baton, the head duck comes in one day and in perfect English says, 'Come here. Something to show you.'

"So I follow him into a larger room where some other men are and they've got rifles and bayonets and there are rats in cages. I mean, the biggest rats you've ever seen, like small dogs, seriously.

"And the head duck says, 'Pick a rat to win.' So I point at a rat, a mean one, and they put it in a cage with another rat and my rat, the one I picked, eats the other rat's eyes right off, first thing. My rat went berserk on the other rat. I won some food and some crappy cigarettes. For a whole week, I picked winning rats. And that was how I stayed alive."

"How did you get out?" I asked.

"I forget," Red Green said. "Someone let me out in the night or something. Don't you see what I'm saying to you?" He stared at me.

I was grinding my teeth. I shook my head. "No," I said. "What are you saying?"

"Pick the right rat, Ray," Red Green said. "I think Dale Carnegie said that."

"Pick the right rat," I repeated.

"Oh, boy," Red Green said. "Never mellow with age, Ray. Resist it at all costs. Stay bitter, in fact. Encourage your own bitter tendencies. Is that what I'm saying?"

"No," I answered. "It doesn't make sense, whatever you're saying."

"Okay," Red Green said. "Now we're getting somewhere. So good luck with all that." He took a swallow from the beer can. "And by good luck, I mean I hope you don't see anything or experience anything that makes you more mental or drives you completely crazy."

"Right," I said. "But you saw it. He was going for his gun."

"Also," Red Green continued, "good luck with the cancer.

You've probably got it already, it's part of life. So I'm wishing you good luck early." He took a swallow of beer. "And don't forget to live your own death in advance, measured with precision, hundreds, thousands of times, every second of some days and before you go to sleep at night, live the hospital, the funeral, I mean, really, dig deep and get it right." He paused to take a quick drag off his cigarette, then continued. "But equally remember that what will always escape you is the suddenness of it, like flicking on a light switch, so in order to get that aspect of it right, try to have the memory of your fake death come to your mind fast, unexpectedly, surprise yourself with it. It won't go the way you try to direct it, you can't get the speed right because it's beyond speed, it's the opposite of speed, it's so slow that it has crept up on you since birth, it just seems fast. And don't confuse a life for being alive. In alive the heart beats. The heart doesn't live its own death. It's the goddamned mind. That's all I have to say, there is nothing else, you've reached the end of my wisdom and I've reached the end of my sharing it with you. I'm sick with the brilliance I've given you, I'm ill from my own speed genius."

"Thanks," I said. "Can't you tell Converse he was reaching for the gun?"

"I wouldn't want to get involved in something so speculative, so uncertain. Then it becomes a whole you-me thing and look where that's gotten us so far. But I will say this. If you ever meet a man who's ninety-six, it's quite obvious he is afraid to die and you can have nothing to do with him. Wayne did not suffer from that fear."

"He was definitely reaching for his gun," I said.

"Hold that point," Red Green said. "And with further

regards to the pre-mentioned good luck, what I mean is that
I hope you get a regular type of cancer, not some weird
untreatable type. Just get regular good old cancer, that's what
you want. Pray for it. Because a friend of mine, not really a
friend but someone I saw on a bus once, he had green bubbles on his head and he said it was from cancer. Unsightly and
incurable, that's a bad combination."

"Right," I said. Converse came in the lab and gave me
some money, told me he'd be in touch if things changed. He
and Red Green stood there, waiting for me to leave. I looked
at Red Green.

"What?" Red Green said. "That's the look you would
give a friend."

"I guess," I said. "We're sort of friends."

"Well you're mental," he said. "I'm not into that."

"I see that now," I said.

"Glad I could be of help," he said. "I'm busy, so you'll
excuse me." He went back to the test tubes and burners. He
waved me good-bye. "Best of luck," he said. "With all of it,
the betrayals, the prison term, the eventual death. I'm root-
ing for you in all things before they happen and I've got big
confidence in you."

"Yes," I said. "I think I understand."

"You're a real piece of hell," he said. "The genuine article."

"Right," I said.

"Are you aware that Master Chan communicated solely
by snapping his fingers for his entire life and that there is a
woman in Ada, Oklahoma, which isn't a town, but a place
where the road widens, a woman who has not been off the
telephone since age eighteen and she is now approaching her
sixtieth birthday? If you don't know things, how can you

ever know other things? Comparison between two facts to create a third, separate thing that may or may not be fact is the basis for much of our philosophic thought today, and that you appear ignorant of that drives me to use drugs to escape you and your low-watt world."

"I didn't know that stuff," I said.

He pointed at the door. "Get out of here," he said. "Your understanding is a puddle so shallow I can't bear it."

"No, seriously," I said. "I understand about the rats and the Shining Path."

Red Green looked at me. "I haven't told the truth in about twelve years," he said. "Any understanding you have about anything is strictly your own invention, a lie you've told yourself about a lie I told you."

Ball Lightning Reported

Two days into a full-on ice storm, I drove the forty-five miles north and east from Burlington to Red Green's house in Newport, Vermont. All along the way, the woods were shattered. Trees splintered from the weight of the ice, scattering limbs and trunks on the frozen snow. Blue sparks arced out of severed high-tension wires, onto the icy blacktop. The temperature shifted by the minute, changing from rain to snow to ice, back to rain. My mind mirrored the storm, fierce addiction raging, beating my brain with baseball-size hailstones of chemical need. I thought about turning around, then thought about getting high at Red's and kept going.

The drive, normally fifty-five minutes in good weather with a crystal meth tailwind, took six hours.

For four years I'd made the drive from Burlington to Newport twice a week. A friend of a friend, that worst of all bridges, had hooked me up with Red again. The friend of a friend mentioned the name and said I should go see Red, that he'd been asking about me.

The first time I saw him again I said, "How'd you find me?"

"I've never lost anything," Red said. "Not a penny, not a memory. Never lost anything. I've gotten rid of some crap, some people, but I don't allow myself to lose things."

I'd just started working at the medical waste facility in South Burlington. Red suggested he might be able to salvage some pharmaceutical-quality drugs from the plastic biohazard containers I stuffed into the industrial autoclave every night. Twice a week, I made sure two full waste containers found their way into the back of my truck.

Red was always happy and so was I—four containers a week paid for all my drugs, mostly a lot of hash and a little hillbilly heroin, OxyContin, with the occasional jolt of some high-octane crank to make sure I functioned during the day. All with as much beer as I could swallow for a chaser. Red stuck to harder stuff than that. Angel dust and liquid cocaine, mixed with dental anesthesia. He was a tweak freak too, and then he'd apply the heroin brakes for a week. The containers I brought would sometimes yield a gold nugget—a half-used bag of morphine, a Haldol drip, or a pound of brightly colored, professional-strength get-high Chiclets. Red had connections and customers for all of it. I never really knew where he got his other stuff. Anybody with crystal meth usually has biker friends, but I never saw any bikers at Red's. Twice weekly, I'd get high at his house, then take the rest of my new stash back to Burlington. Four years of this arrangement had bumped me up to angel dust and meth, until I needed heroin to dampen the evil hum that became my internal theme music.

The storm peaked as I reached the outskirts of Newport, ice pellets machine-gunning the truck's windshield under huge, irregular booms of thunder. Red Green's house sat on the edge of Lake Memphremagog. I followed the old shore road around the giant frozen lake until I was in front of his house, a one-level, white shack with a concrete block for a step and pink insulation stuffed inside the windows. As I got out of the truck, I pulled up the collar of my barn jacket against the ice pellets and made a dash for the back door, which faced the lake. I could smell woodsmoke. Thunder boomed and lightning struck the lake a hundred yards from the back porch. Right where the bolt hit, I saw three balls of glowing, crackling light. The balls rose slow off the ice and traveled about thirty feet, each one hissing and spitting and fading, until they dissipated into nothing. The sight-echo of three bright spots stayed on my eyes.

I opened the back porch door. Red was lying on the couch wearing a dirty flannel shirt and a pair of jeans, with logger's boots. The fireplace was going full blast, the flames providing the only light in the room. As close to the fire as he could get without being burned was a long, short-haired dog. He was pretty big, close to a hundred pounds. He had a blanket over his butt and he was shaking, his collar and tags jingling. The dog was a new addition since my last visit. I nodded at Red and he pointed to the table on my left. I pulled a chair out and sat down and smoked a fair amount of hash and angel dust before I turned to speak to him.

"What's wrong with your dog?" I asked.

"He can't stand the cold, and thunder makes him nervous," Red answered. We both looked at the dog, still shaking under the blanket close to the fire.

"What kind of dog is he?" I wondered.

"Rhodesian ridgeback," Red said.

I shook my head. "Never heard of that."

Red pointed to the floor and I noticed a stack of books, all with identical blue bindings. "Look it up. I got some encyclopedias the other day. A guy knocked on the front door and said he was selling them. I got him high and he gave me a set."

I looked at Red. "He was really selling encyclopedias door-to-door out here, in this weather?"

Red shook his head. "He wasn't selling encyclopedias door-to-door. He was selling these encyclopedias. He bought them for his wife and now she ran off to Florida, so he wanted to get rid of them. He's local, I've seen him before— you'd know him if you saw him. He's got big bucked teeth. I think his name is Dixon."

I moved to the floor and looked at the encyclopedias. I pulled out the letter *R* and leafed through it. Under the entry "Rhodesian ridgeback," there was a picture of Red's dog.

"What does it say?" Red asked.

"Those dogs were bred to hunt lions. Some people call them The Lion Dog. They have a ridge of fur on their back."

I crawled over toward the fire and examined the dog's back. A sharp line of short fur, pointing up from the rest of his coat, rode directly along the dog's backbone. I read further in the encyclopedia. "It says that Rhodesia doesn't exist anymore. This calls it 'the former Rhodesia.'"

Red thought for a moment. "That's true about a lot of things," he said. He leaned forward and snorted some whitish powder off the coffee table in front of him.

I looked at the R volume closely. "Encyclopaedia Britannica" was engraved on the front cover, in cheap gold script. Stamped in the middle of the spine was the letter R. At the top of the spine, written in gold, was the year 1985. Some of the other books had different years stamped on them and slightly different covers. "These are old," I said. "These aren't new. They're no good. Some of them are from different years."

Red picked up a beer bottle from the coffee table, took a long drink, and set it back down among the other, empty bottles. He shook his head. "What difference does that make, as long as they're all there? The letters are all there. How can they be no good?"

"They aren't accurate. The information is old, and anything that happened after eighty-five is missing." I crawled over to the pile of encyclopedias and put R back on top.

"Stuff doesn't change that much," said Red. "Read me something that's changed. Start at the beginning, find A, and read me something that's changed a lot." He snorted more powder off the coffee table.

I found A and opened to the first page of text. "Okay. Here's something that's changed a lot."

"Read it to me."

Outside, the storm wailed.

I cleared my throat. "It's information about alcoholism, but they have this side story, about how this guy got sent to Eastern Oklahoma Hospital for the Insane and how they made him bite on a raw steak while they gave him electro-shock therapy."

Red looked at me. "How has that changed? People still do that. I know people that have gone to the hospital for drinking."

"No. Alcoholism treatment has changed a lot."

Red shrugged. "They do the same thing today, but with different drugs." Then he nodded. "Okay, that's a change, they don't talk about modern drugs. But that's not a big change. They still put alkies in the bughouse." He stood and went to the kitchen. I heard him open the fridge. When he walked back into the living room, he had a raw steak in his mouth. The dog stared at him.

"What are you doing?" I said.

He talked around the steak, muffled. "In case I get shocked." Blood from the steak dripped on his chin and shirt. "Life is shocking." He took it out of his mouth and flipped it to the dog. It didn't seem to last three bites.

"Electroshock therapy," I said. "That can kill you." I nodded at the encyclopedias. "It's out-of-date."

"Okay. They're out-of-date." Red nodded. "Okay, that's pretty bad. But I'm telling you, even today, if they get you into one of those nuthouses, you're in for it." He took a drink of beer. "Those posh rehabs you see on TV are for movie stars. Don't kid yourself—scum like us get sent to lockdown joints. The rich men get ice in the summer and the poor men get ice in the winter, but don't tell me that's an even break."

"But the electric shocks could be worse than the drinking," I said.

Red nodded. "Okay, that doesn't sound so good. When I'm high I'm high, but when I'm not, I'm not. The shit doesn't carry over from one day to the next unless I get high again. Therefore," he finished, "I do not battle demon addiction." He listened to the storm and pointed at the books. "At least I've got a full set." He looked over at me. "Find *F,* and look up faro."

I came up with *F.* "What's faro?"

"An old-time card game." He drank some beer.

I found faro. "Here it is. It says, 'Card game played with an ordinary fifty-two-card deck, by any number of persons, for the sole purpose of gambling.'" A brief set of rules followed.

"A new encyclopedia wouldn't have that. That's an old-time game." He nodded. "My mother used to talk about faro. See, that's worth something right there."

I shook my head. "But important stuff is missing." I leafed through *F.* The two Fords listed were Henry and Gerald. "It doesn't even have President Ford's wife getting sober. Or him getting shot at."

Red sniffed more powder off the coffee table. "What do I care about him? He's dead."

"No he isn't. See, that's what I mean, stuff is missing." We sat silent. I got up and snorted some more dust, all up my right nostril. The dog was still shaking.

"As long as I've got a full set, that's all I care about," Red said.

I decided to tell him about the ball lightning. "Hey, know what I saw coming in here?"

Red shook his head.

"Ball lightning," I said.

"What's that?"

I crawled back over to the encyclopedias. "I'll look it up. My father used to talk to me about it, how lightning can travel in a ball if the weather is right." The *B* volume didn't have an entry for ball lightning.

"Try weather," Red suggested. "See, if you'd been struck, I could have helped you out with that steak."

"I'll try meteorology," I said. I started to go through *M*.

Red sipped a beer. "What day is it?" he asked.

"I don't know," I said. I could tell Red was headed for a weird altitude, either going up or coming down, I couldn't quite tell which.

"I think it's my mother's birthday."

I nodded. "You should call her."

"I tried before, but the phones are out," he responded.

"Where does your mom live?" I asked.

"She used to live in Reno. She likes to gamble," he said. "But I think she moved to Toronto. I should go visit her."

"You could wish her happy birthday," I said.

"How much does a ticket to Toronto cost?" he asked.

"I'll look it up," I said and pawed through the encyclopedias. *T* was missing. "Red, *T*'s missing."

"That guy was such an asshole. I fucking said to him, 'Are they all there?' and he said, 'Oh, yeah, all the letters.' What a bastard!" Red got off the couch and started to pace around. "You better go. Leave. Lately, when I start to come down, shit gets ugly. I'll catch you later."

"But the storm—" I started.

"I don't give a fucking damnhell about the storm!" His face was inflamed and his eyes narrowed. His words slammed around. "You're leaving. Now!"

I got off the floor and walked out the back door. It was raining a little, thunder rumbling in the distance. Red followed me. I heard him mumble "fucking Dixon" as he reached the porch.

"Hey," he said. "Help me with the snowmobile. I can drive to see my mother."

Parked next to the house was a snowmobile. I took the scraper out of my truck and started smacking ice off the seat. Red came back with a kitchen knife and knocked most of the ice off the dashboard. He sat on the seat and turned the key. The engine sputtered and coughed, then stayed running. The headlight came on. Red whooped.

"Fucking shit works!" he said. He pointed straight ahead, over the icy lake. "That's Canada, right?"

I mouthed "yes" over the now-roaring engine.

"Here I go," he said. "The former Red Green." He put his hands on the steering handles and gunned the throttle. The snowmobile jumped forward, then gained speed toward the lake, leaving a choppy trail from its single belt track. Red flew—out over the ice, faster, until he was eighty yards off-shore. The snowmobile broke through the frozen surface and the machine disappeared into the water, taking Red down with it, under the ice. I stared at where he'd been, the hole. A faint glow from the snowmobile's taillights filtered up through the ice, then faded. I knelt on the frozen snow as my high started to really kick in. I saw the ridgeback standing on the back porch. The dog opened its mouth to bark, but what came out was my voice, screaming.

I woke up facedown in the snow, covered with a thick layer of ice. My face was raw and tight. The trail of the snowmobile led out onto the lake and abruptly stopped near a newly frozen patch. I shook myself off and climbed into my truck. The ridgeback came out of the house when the engine turned over. I opened the passenger's door and he hopped in, shaking from the cold.

I drove back to Burlington. The road was the same going in as it had been coming out, except that I was suddenly alive, with a desire to stay that way. I never actually saw ball lightning again, although I know it occurs from time to time.

Controlled Burn

After a bad winter and a worse spring, came the summer Bill Allen lived and died, the sweltering summer I landed a job cutting trees for Robert Wilson's scab-logging outfit near Orford, New Hampshire. June boiled itself away into the heavy steam of July. Heat devils rose in waves off the blacktop as timber trucks rolled in. By the end of July, we switched gears and started cutting stove wood. I was cutting eight cords a day while Robert worked the hydraulic splitter. Then we'd deliver it in one of our dump trucks. Men also drove to the woodlot to pick up their own. Some of them had white salt marks on their boots and jackets from sweat. Some of them smelled like beer. Most smelled like gasoline. They didn't say much, just paid for their wood and left with it in their pickup trucks. They were either busy working or busy living their lies, which is work in itself. I knew about that. The hard work crushed one empty beer can day after another, adding to my lifetime pile of empties. Summer moved on, gray in spite of the sun.

That Friday, I was Bill Allen. I was Bill Allen all that summer. Bill Allen was what caused me to jump every time the phone rang. I was Bill Allen from Glens Falls, New York, and I was taking a summer off from college. I repeated that story as often and as loudly as possible. And each ring of the phone might be someone asking me to prove I was Bill Allen, which was out of the question. Back in December, in the middle of another, different lie, I tried to rob a gas station near Cape May, New Jersey. It was off-season then, nobody around, and I thought it would be easy. It fit the person I'd lied about being. A high school girl was behind the counter. I wore a ski mask and carried a cheap semiautomatic pistol. I must have touched the trigger, because the gun went off. Maybe she lived. I hope so but I really couldn't say. The cash register exploded from the bullet and she screamed. I took a roll of bills and left fast. People that scream aren't dead, or at least that's what I repeated to myself a million times. My brain was on fire, I hadn't meant to shoot her. But it was too late for that. I ended up at Robert's. He paid cash at the end of the week, didn't bother with Uncle Sam, didn't ask for references and without his son around to help him, had plenty of backbreaking work that needed doing. Bill Allen was just the man for the job, and every day, I was Bill Allen to the best of my ability. It didn't help. I watched every car, studied every face in the Connecticut River Valley. Bill Allen never knew a peaceful day. If it hadn't been for the marathon workload Robert demanded, Bill Allen never would have slept. I'd have probably shot Bill Allen myself, if I hadn't been working so hard to keep him going. These days he lives on with different names. Allen Williams, Al Wilson, Bill Roberts. Bill Allen probably died in a fire that summer. Leave it at that, with questions about Bill Allen.

The phone at the woodlot rang around noon that Friday. I heard it, had been hearing it most of August. Robert's son John was in jail in Concord, awaiting trial for murderous assault, so there were a lot of phone calls. Robert had rigged the phone with two speakers—one bolted to the stovepipe that stuck out of the roof of our headquarters shack, and the other attached by some baling wire to the sick elm on the end of the lot. The sudden scream of the phone spiked my heart rate at least twice a day, echoing in the alleys between the giant piles of long logs. The woodlot sat surrounded by low, field-grass hills and trees in a natural bowl, just off the highway north of Hanover. Robert's house was on the top of the hill, built with its back to the woodlot, facing a farm field. On a still day, the beauty of the Connecticut River drifted the quarter mile over the farm field and quietly framed all the other sounds, the birds, the trees in the breeze. I was never a part of those days.

The phone rang over the diesel roar of my yellow Maxi-Lift, the near dead cherry picker we kept around to police up the yard. I was working, sweating in the sun, busy shifting a full twelve-ton load of New Hampshire rock maple onto

the drying mountains of timber, heat against next year's
winter. The phone rang again, not that anyone wanted to
talk to me. Most times, I'd shut the equipment down, run
across the yard, slam into the shed, pick up and get "Robert
there?" and they'd hang up when I said no. Or they wouldn't
say anything, just hang up when they knew I wasn't Robert.
And I could breathe again, because it wasn't someone looking for me. Just locals, as if I couldn't take a wood order. Or
it would be the mechanical jail operator, would I please
accept a collect call from inmate John Wilson at the Merri-
mack Correctional Facility. Then I'd say yes and have to go
get Robert anyway. Nobody wanted to talk to me, and I
didn't want to talk to anyone, so I let it ring. Robert would
get it. Or he wouldn't. They know where to find me, he'd
say. Working in the same place for thirty years, if they can't
find me, what the hell would I want to talk to them for, he'd
say. Must be stupid if they can't get hold of me. Robert's
voice was heavy and low, carrying years of cigarettes, muck-
ing up the inside of his barrel chest. There was no sign at the
dirt road entrance to the woodlot. It was Robert Wilson's
woodlot and everyone knew that without asking.

Robert came out of the shed and waved at me to shut the
cherry picker down. I flipped a switch, turned the keys back
a click and cranked the brake on. I walked over to the shed.
Robert had his jean coveralls on. He squinted against the
sun, nodded, and spoke.

"That was Frank Lord. He wants his wood tomorrow."
Robert took twenty-five dollars out of his pocket and handed
it to me. That was our deal—fifty dollars if I had to work on
Saturday, twenty-five up front. "You can fix his load today."

I shrugged. "What does he get?"

"Two cord, plus a half a cord of kiln-dried."

Robert had converted an old single-wide trailer into a kiln and most of his customers ordered mixed loads of both air- and kiln-dried. Kiln-dried wood burns hotter than air-dried. Mixing a kiln-dried log in with every fire produces more heat, allows the air-dried wood to burn more efficiently. People with woodstoves get as much heat out of two air-dried cords mixed with a half cord of kiln-dried as people who burn four straight cords. When a single woodstove is the primary heat source for a whole house, each log has to do its job. Robert charged more for kiln-dried and nobody kicked about the price.

I took my Texaco ball cap off. "If you don't want it mixed, we'll have to take two trucks." Lord's farm was thirty-five miles north and slightly west, just on the Vermont side of the Connecticut River, near Newbury. The river came straight down through the Northeast Kingdom and just past Wells River, where it made an oxbow, flowing briefly north in a U-shaped collar, before returning to its southern course. Lord's farm encompassed all of the Oxbow, stretching from Route Five all the way east to the river, the Vermont–New Hampshire border. The most beautiful spot on earth, the most amazing fields and woods and sky that Bill Allen had ever seen. Robert and I had driven past once that summer, on the way to Wells River to pick up a chain saw. Looking out of the truck as we drove up Route Five and seeing Lord's white farm buildings and fields, I thought maybe I could make it through Bill Allen and still have a life, somewhere. On the way back, the view of the green fields sweeping out into the bend of the river made everything stop. I didn't hear the engine, or the gears. We floated along the road as my mind took picture after picture, of the farm and the fields and the blue sky with the setting sun. That bend in the river. I came alive for a minute and as the farm slowly passed by, I died again, back into the zombie lie of Bill Allen.

Robert was talking to me, shaking his head. "He's got some extra work. Stobe can drive the small rig."

Stobik lived south of the woodlot, in White River Junction, and did odd jobs for Robert. He didn't have a phone—if Robert needed him for something, I'd drive down first thing in the morning and pick him up. Just pull my beat-up Bronco into his dooryard and sit there till he came out. Sometimes, a thin, white hand would appear in the dirty window, waving me away. Too drunk to work. He had lived in a rain culvert on the woodlot for about a month when things got tough with his wife. She was as big as the house they lived in. He was skinny as a rail, hadn't showered in about a week, month, year. His teeth were broken brown stumps and his fingers were stained from tobacco. But he could cut and stack firewood faster than two men, and at half the price.

"I'll pick him up in the morning," I said.

"That's okay. I'll get him tonight and let him sleep on the porch," Robert said. "I want to make sure he can work tomorrow." He walked back inside the shed. I fixed Frank Lord's load of wood for the next day and went to the barn loft I called home.

Next morning, I was at the woodlot at five-thirty. It was pitch black. Robert was already there, sitting in his pickup truck, drinking coffee and eating a hard-boiled egg. He had the running lights on. I drove slowly over to the open driver's side window.

"Thought you overslept," he said.

I climbed out of the Bronco and sat shotgun in the big white rig. Stobik got behind the wheel of the small one.

The floor of the white rig was taken up with logging chains. The last job Robert had used it for was a semi-commercial haul and he'd left the chains in. He had a whole barn full of them up by his house. He'd load them in the truck and then get weighed, toss them out at the job and then leave them there. The customer paid the difference. How many people paid for those chains, only God knows. The fuse box was open on the passenger's side, so any metal that jumped up during the ride could cause a spark or worse. It made for a tense ride.

We started the drive up to North Haverhill on the New Hampshire side of the Connecticut River. The truck could only make thirty-five fully loaded. Stobik sat right behind us, with the flashers on. Robert wrestled the gears up a hill. Then he lit a cigarette and spoke.

"When I was fifteen, I ran away and ended up on Frank Lord's farm." He looked over at me.

"I didn't know that," I answered.

"Frank Lord worked me so hard I thought I was going to drop. But it straightened me out. Best thing that ever happened to me."

"What was wrong with you?" I asked.

"Bad temper," Robert answered. We passed a broken-down barn. "Bad temper and drinking."

"At fifteen?"

Robert nodded. "Back then, fifteen was like thirty-five.

You had a job, a car—they made you live life back then and if you didn't like it, get the fuck out." He took a drag off his cigarette. He was silent, smoking, for the rest of the ride.

Frank Lord stood in his driveway as we pulled up. He had an oxygen mask on and a green tank marked OXYGEN in white letters standing next to him. The fields stretched out behind him all the way to the river. His big white farmhouse needed a coat of paint. There were a couple of barns and outbuildings. They needed paint, too. Alongside of the main house rested a brand-new pickup truck. On top of the main house perched a black wrought-iron weather vane, the silhouette of a big black stallion. The weather vane pointed north.

He saw Robert and half-waved. "What are you going to do, make something out of yourself or what?" His voice was muffled behind the clear plastic mask. His breath filled it with mist. He pointed over toward the nearest barn. "Put the wood over there," he said through the mask. "Don't mix it together."

He and Robert walked slowly toward the main house and sat on the porch in kitchen chairs. Stobik and I unloaded and stacked the wood. Stobik worked fast. His stacks were the straightest I've ever seen. His face seemed frozen in a perpetual grin as we worked in silence. The stacks came out perfectly. We went back over to Robert and Frank on the porch. It was just around noon.

"I did all the work," I said.

Robert nodded to Stobik. "I can tell who's the horse and who's the jackass."

"We've got some other work to do," Frank said. He held out a piece of paper.

"What's that?" I asked.

"Yesterday, in the morning, Judge Harris stopped over here. Unofficially. I've known his family for probably, oh, fifty years." The breeze tossed the tops of the corn. "He told me that the state police got a tip I was growing marijuana. They were trying to get a warrant to search my house and my fields." He held out the paper. "Harris dropped this off." I read the paper. It was a one-day special permit for a controlled burn.

"What do you want us to do?" I asked.

"Burn it, all of it. Right back to the river. I don't want a single thing left alive." He stared straight at Stobik and me. "Just in case there's a little Mexican hay that got mixed in with my corn somehow."

Robert came down off the porch to supervise. We started at the front of the field closest to the farm, with the wind blowing toward the river. He and I rigged up a sprayer with some gas and soaked a good portion of the front field. We left a wide strip in the middle completely dry. In between the rows of corn, planted in groups of three, stood the pot plants that Frank Lord made his money from.

Then we drove the tractor through a thin line of trees and there was a huge cornfield that stretched all the way to the river. In the middle of the field, probably six hundred yards away, stood a small white shack.

Robert spoke up. "That's where my first wife and I lived." He stared at it.

I glanced over at him. "I never think about you being married."

He nodded. "Well I was, for a while." He pointed at the shack. "People that live in places like that don't very often stay married." He studied the white shack. "I had a bad temper then."

I rubbed my eyes. "Should we burn it?"

"Oh yeah." Robert wiped his forehead with a red kerchief. Sweat had run down from his forehead and got into his eyes and on his chin.

I looked over at the white shack. "What if there are people in it?"

"Then fuck 'em, let 'em burn. Their name isn't Lord and they don't belong on this property." Robert pulled at a cornstalk. "Frank said burn it, and that's what we're going to do." He looked across the rows of corn toward the river. "Hotter than Hades." He looked over at me. "You'll never be cold again, after this." He started to drive the tractor toward the white shack with me on the back of his seat. "Here, watch this," he shouted over the tractor.

We pulled up next to the shack. The windows on our side had been broken, but the chicken wire in the glass remained, rusted from the weather. I heard a faint hum.

"Watch," Robert said. He took the nozzle from the gas sprayer and aimed a fine stream at the window. I saw wasps beginning to fly out of the broken window. They moved slowly, clinging to the chicken wire. Robert pointed at them and talked above the noise of the tractor. I could see their insect heads, sectioned bodies, and stingers. They were getting soaked with gas. "Throw a match," he said.

"No," I told him. "It'll explode." I pointed at the sprayer and the tank of gas on the tractor.

"Gas doesn't burn," Robert said. "It's wet. Nothing that's wet can burn. It's the fumes that burn." He took a wood match out of his pocket and struck it on the tractor, then tossed the small flame into the gas spray.

The air groaned and came alive with fire. The wasps were

flying full-bore out of the broken window now, right into the wall of flame and through it. Their wings caught fire, still beating, the air currents lifting them up in the heat even as they burned to nothing. A flaming wasp landed on my work shirt and I smacked it into the corn. Now they were everywhere, burning and flying. Stinging anything they touched. One lost a wing and kept flying, a coin-size flaming circle into the corn. I watched one come out of the window whole, coated shiny with gas. It flew over the corn; its wings caught fire and kept beating as the body burned to a cinder, the wings still going until they vanished in tiny ash. Robert smacked some wasps off his arm and pulled the tractor up, driving forward to the river.

We soaked the corn next to the river and then sprayed it a little thinner up on the bank. "The fire will seek the gas," Robert said. "That patch we left in the middle will burn slower than the rest. We'll be all set."

We decided that the best way to do it was to have Stobik drive the truck around to the New Hampshire side of the Oxbow. Then I'd light the fire from the riverbank, so that the onrushing flames wouldn't somehow jump the river. Robert drove the tractor back through the field, leaving me standing right on the bend in the river with a box of matches. I could barely see the white shack over the corn. The river ran behind me, softly laughing its way over the rocks. Everything was still and my heart almost stopped panting for the first time in a long while. Bill Allen stood on the riverbank and knew he needed to die. He knew he had to go back to the place he was born and answer for the crime that had fathered him. I heard the air horn blow from the big rig, Robert's signal to me that he was clear of the fields. As I lit the corn on fire, Bill Allen decided to throw himself into the blaze. I had no intention of killing myself, just trying to find my way back to normal life, no matter how painful that might be. I had formed my own truth out of lies and I needed to get rid of that.

The flames grew fast and I jumped out into the Connecticut River. It must have been cool, but I didn't feel it. The heat from the fire seemed to reach across the Oxbow and right through the water. I climbed up on the bank on the other side just in time to see Robert's white wedding shack take the flames full force. The walls and roof caught like they were made of rice paper and in the next instant, the shack was gone. The fire was so hot I couldn't look at it. I walked further up on the bank, where Stobik stood with the small truck. I got in and we started to drive back toward Vermont. A black cloud rose against the beautiful blue horizon and we watched it for miles. It seemed we'd permanently smudged the sky.

When we got back to Lord's farm, Robert was busy fending off several local volunteer fire companies who had arrived with sirens and lights going. He just kept showing them the permit Judge Harris had given to Frank.

One of the firemen, a solid-looking local guy, held the permit in his hand. "Mister Lord," he said, "what the hell are you up to? Controlled burn? Those two words don't even go together." He lectured Robert and Frank Lord on the dangers of fire. He was right.

Stobik and I stayed in the small truck. At one point, I swear the flames in the field were higher than the farmhouse. Stobik backed the truck up so the windshield wouldn't crack. I finally got out and sat alone in the passenger's side of the big rig. I fell asleep. It was late that night when Robert climbed in to drive and slammed his door, bringing me straight up in my seat. The fields were still burning. We drove slowly back to the woodlot and I slept there in my Bronco. The next day, Sunday, I was going to drive all day and turn myself in. Bill Allen was dead.

The screaming echo of the phone over the woodlot woke me. I saw Robert go into the headquarters shack to answer it. He came back out shortly, still in his coveralls, and walked to the Bronco. I got out. He handed me a styrofoam cup of coffee and pointed at the Bronco.

"Comfy in there last night?" he asked. I nodded and sipped the coffee and he went on. "That was John on the phone. He's going to plead out tomorrow and take two years." Robert shook his head. "Anyway, you've got tomorrow off. I'm going up to Concord to be at the sentencing." He reached in his pocket and pulled out a big roll of bills. He handed it to me.

"What's this for?" I said.

Robert narrowed his eyes and looked at me. "Do you need it or not?" His voice was the hardest love I'd ever felt. I nodded. He turned around and started walking back to the shed. I watched him close the door. I climbed back in the Bronco and headed out onto the highway. I drove north, and crossed into Vermont. There was still a huge black cloud in the sky over the Oxbow. I rode Route Five and the burnt fields were still smoldering, scorched dead. Lord's farm had taken on the gray from the smoke. I drove up into the Northeast Kingdom and spent the winter at a logging camp in Quebec. I never did find the courage to turn myself in and things got worse.

*   *   *

I called the woodlot once, when I hit a jam out in North
Dakota. Standing in a phone booth, outside a diner, I recognized John's voice the second he spoke. I hung up. Later,
much later, in another life, with another name, we were driving around and someone handed me a road atlas. I flipped
through it and found Vermont and New Hampshire together
on the same page. I started tracing their shared border, the
Connecticut River, north toward Canada. My finger reached
the Oxbow. For just that split second, right on the tip of my
finger, the surface of the map was scorching hot. I heard the
roar of the fire, the little white house burning. The air rushing to be eaten by the flames. I smelled the gasoline. Riding
across the top of the fire on a black horse was Bill Allen.
Three dark shapes followed swiftly after him, burning wasps
caught in their long black hair, chasing him. Catching him
and dragging him down into the fire, screaming.

Years later, on the security ward at Western State Hospital
near Tacoma, I saw a man in a straitjacket, strapped to a gur-
ney. I walked over to him.

"Didn't know they used straitjackets anymore."

He could barely move his head. "Well, they do." The smell
of ether was everywhere. He stayed quiet as a white-jacketed
doctor walked by. "Say, Mac, scratch my shoulder, will you?"

I slowly reached down and began scratching the outside
of the thick canvas that bound him. Solid steel mesh covered
the ward windows.

"Harder," he said. "I can barely feel it." He looked up at
me. "I think they're trying to save on heat. Aren't you cold?"
I shook my head. "I'm cold all the time," he said.

I dug my nails into the canvas on his right shoulder. "My name is John Wilson," I said.

He looked at me, his eyes wide. "That's my name," he said softly.

I stopped scratching the straitjacket. "What's your middle name?" I asked.

He shook his head slightly and closed his eyes. "Same as yours," he said. He shivered. It was cold. But my paper gown was soaked with dry sweat and my face was hot. I could smell smoke.

Tigers

for RH
& AJC

People say ice is not alive, yet it grows. Ice eats the cold off the air and makes itself thicker and stronger and everywhere. Above thirty-two degrees, ice begins to die back into water. Continent-size glaciers vanish for want of a single digit of cooler air. Then the cold returns and ice is born again, alive.

That winter morning, all up and down the Connecticut River Valley, temperatures rose above the normal freeze and people in the small parking lot at Dan and Whit's in Norwich said they heard pond ice cracking so loud they thought it was gunshots. There was a fatal accident at the freight-loading dock in White River Junction as a pallet of gas stoves, stacked too high, tipped and fell onto the workers standing on the dock below. On a curve coming into Hanover, a car clipped a utility pole as it skidded off the road. Electricity and phone service flickered till noon, as if the whole valley were slipping and sliding. The ice from the river crept onto the road and across driveways and died into water and then lived again.

North of Hanover, a mile south of the Orford corner, three old farm mansions sat back two hundred yards off the snow-covered road. Mark Hoff's job was at the middle house. A storm passing through had ripped the tops out of two full-grown pines, close to the house. Ten feet of one top leaned on the gutter. The trees were seventy feet tall apiece and the owner was lucky to still have a roof.

Mark stayed there all day with his earplugs and glasses on, running the saw until both stumps were flat and smooth, as close to the ground as he could make them. He'd be back to grind them in the spring. Fifteen years, since he got out of high school, Mark had been cutting trees. Locally and as far north as Quebec a few years ago, as an independent contractor clearing power lines after a storm. The big outfit to work for in New England was Galvin's Tree Service, with a full crew assigned to each bucket truck and lots of contracts. Mark liked things the way they were, just him and his truck. He didn't think he'd last with a big outfit or a boss other than himself.

The kitchen curtain moved a couple times as he was cutting, and he caught the motion with the edge of his eye. He wanted a cup of coffee, but also didn't want to stop working. In the cold, coffee was good going down, it warmed you up.

Then you had to piss. That was no good on residential jobs, where the owners were watching. He didn't want to offend anyone. The curtain moved again. He hated being watched as he worked, although he knew they all did it. He pushed the homeowner out of his mind.

Instead, he thought about Ann Latham, eighteen months his girlfriend, and Jimmy, Ann's son, and he hurried without being sloppy, to finish. He was sweating under his jacket, as he walked the fallen trees, limbing them neatly. The trees lay cut into ten-foot lengths, ready to be picked up by the cherry picker driver who Mark contracted with. Sawdust covered the frozen crust of snow and pine chips in the driveway by the time he finished, resting the big Jonsered in the bed of his truck. The powerful saw was perfect for residential work and for the logging jobs he bid up in the Northeast Kingdom. The right side of the saw was flat because of an inboard clutch, so limb work was easy. The handles and carburetor were electrically heated to beat the cold. If his saw wasn't running, he was out of business and he couldn't afford that. He was happy with the job the saw had done today.

The Orbachs had owned the place for years—he'd cut a tree for them—but the new owner's name was Judith Selmann, and she came shivering out into the driveway to pay Mark three hundred dollars before he left, a hundred and fifty per tree, with a check drawn on a Manhattan bank. Which did him no good at all, as it was Friday and the check wouldn't clear till at least Tuesday.

After he got the check, Mark said, "Hey, don't watch me so hard. I know what I'm doing." Judith Selmann was about to say something but Mark turned away and walked to his truck, still talking, half to himself. "Cut trees here before you owned it." He started his truck and pulled onto the highway.

He drove through Hanover, around the green in front of Dartmouth, and into Lebanon, depositing the check and taking out a hundred dollars for the weekend. He lived three miles north of Hanover on the first floor of the house that had been his grandfather's. His younger brother lived on the second floor and drove a route truck for White Mountain Fuel Oil.

When Mark woke up Saturday morning, his head was pounding and full of snot and it was hard to breathe. He called Ann's house in Lebanon. Ann was an office manager for an ophthalmologist. She was working all day and her sister was watching Jimmy. Mark left a message on Ann's machine, thinking about his tone because his habit was to be short with people on the phone. He tried to be upbeat, light. She didn't have to come over if she didn't want to. He was sick and probably wouldn't be much fun, but he'd still buy the pizza if she wanted to come by. And that he loved her. He ended the message with "I love you." Then he hung up and went to sleep.

Love is alive. It grows and can be found in a lot of places. Love needs much attention to keep growing, but when alive, it is a beautiful thing.

In the late afternoon, Mark got up and made sure the door was unlocked. He walked through the house in his socks. Put a log in the stove. Took a drink of orange juice from the fridge and went back to sleep. About six-thirty, he heard the two of them coming up the walk, the click of her steps sounding even in the snow and the little boy following and asking questions. The door opened and they were in.

"How's the best boy in the world?" Mark called from the bedroom.

"He wasn't around," Ann called back. "But I found this little boy on the side of the road and brought him instead. He seems like a pretty good little boy."

Mark heard the smile in her voice without seeing her face. They were taking off their boots and coats near the front door. "How's the world's best mom?"

"Ask her when you see her," Ann answered. "I'm so tired I'll be asleep on the couch when she gets here."

Jimmy was busy with his silent inspection of the pipes and the water in the house, bathroom and kitchen, toilet and sink, and then making sure his own mini-armchair was in just the right place by Mark's bedroom door. When the ritual was complete, Jimmy sat in the chair, clutching his stuffed tiger. He sat staring at Mark, the picture of the perfect child in his tan corduroy pants, sneakers, and blue turtleneck. The doctors described Jimmy's problems as an obsessive desire for the preservation of sameness. Mark had heard several different doctors, in fact, use those same words, that phrase. It made Ann cry. But only once. She didn't cry about it anymore, when they went to see the doctors together. Jimmy's father was a long-haul trucker and he wasn't in the picture, except for the occasional child-support payment. Sometimes the checks came and sometimes they didn't. Ann deserved better, she deserved regularity, like all single moms. Maybe the real world didn't allow for better, could only fit in one man driving his rig from

Fresno to Tallahassee to Cleveland to Austin to Baltimore all within a week, sending money when he had it.

Mark breathed in and out. "Hear that?" he asked Jimmy. The popping and wheezing in his breath sounded like animals howling in the night. "It sounds like coyotes got into my throat."

"And a tiger," Jimmy said.

"Of course," Mark said. "A throat tiger."

Jimmy sat in his mini-chair until the pizza arrived and then Ann gave it to him, on a paper plate, one slice at a time. She ate a piece too and then drove home with Jimmy, before she got too tired. She kissed Mark on the forehead before she left. He listened to her footsteps in the snow, out to her car, the muffled closing of the doors and the engine starting, then moving itself away. Sick as he was, Mark thought he could work hard enough to do this, to repeat this scene Saturdays into the future, as far as he could see. They arranged themselves in front of him, weekends to be worked for, whole seasons, summers, a string of Christmases. Mark wanted his hard work to count for something. A family. This family. Families were alive, to Mark. If anyone had asked him, he'd have talked for a long time about families. Nobody asked Mark much, except prices to take trees down and how much they owed him for the wood he delivered.

He recovered some of his health over the course of Sunday and was back behind the saw Monday morning, cutting more trees near Orford in the freezing cold. Thinking about Ann and Jimmy. Wanting, in his own way, the same thing Jimmy wanted. He didn't want to spend his life working for nothing.

*   *   *

Tigers are alive. They are everywhere, from Detroit to Bengal to the cereal aisle in the grocery store, and they are big and strong, some eighteen feet in length. Those are two of the things you need for being alive, to be strong and to be everywhere. Any real circus has tigers and they bring them across the country because people sometimes like to see real live jungle tigers, not just read about Pooh Bear and his friend. Jungle tigers live in cages at night, even in the real jungle, because in a cage, if it's a big cage and you lock the door from the inside, no one can bother you. Tigers are alive and friendly and dangerous all at once.

Local men and women who work hard and who are loyal think hard about things while they work. They don't need to think about what street to turn down or when the bank closes, because they've done it so many times. Local men and women think about health and money. Pictures of kids in their wallets, sons and daughters in the service and in college. Pictures of grandkids. Local men and women think about health and money. They think about small things that changed the course of a day or a week or even a year. Years later, thinking back to when he first met Jimmy, Mark spent a lot of time dwelling on that very first night. So the night, the memory of the night, became part of Mark's everyday routine, grew into something much more than a memory.

He never knew what changed her mind that night, was never certain. Ann wanted to go to dinner and Mark wanted to take her. But his truck smelled like gas and chain saw oil.

He borrowed a car from his buddy George Post. Mark and George had cleared some poolrooms in their high school days and after. Not anymore, work didn't allow for it. George got booted from the Navy and worked for his father as a plumber's helper. The car was a four-door Pontiac sedan, a leftover from George's grandfather, so it smelled faintly of White Owl cigars and always would. Mark parked in front of George's house and they walked around to the detached garage. The Pontiac was light green.

"It's a bed with wheels," George said. He patted the long hood. "This backseat has seen some real action."

"Not tonight," Mark said.

"So you say," George said. He gave Mark the keys. "Tank's full," he said. "Have fun."

Maybe what changed Ann's mind was Mark borrowing the car. It was nice to get into a vehicle that didn't smell like gas and oil, with a seat that she didn't have to check for grease so as not to stain her clothes. Maybe it was because Mark opened all the doors for her that night, she looked so beautiful. Maybe it was the wheel skirts on the Pontiac. Ann's short, dark hair was perfect. Her skin glowed, her smile was bright, and her eyes sparkled. Maybe it was the way they talked over dinner or the way Mark paid the check, smooth and easy. Maybe it was because he wore a crisp white shirt and khakis, instead of jeans. Maybe it was because they didn't have sex in the car that night. Maybe it was none of those things. Mark and Ann had a ritual. He usually dropped her at the end of her street and watched her walk to the door of her house. She was careful, with her son and the men he met in her life. But this time Ann said, "Why don't you park in front tonight, if you'd like to meet Jimmy."

Mark nodded. "I'd like that." He kept nodding. "We've talked about him so much, I'd like to meet him."

"Fine," Ann said. "Tonight's a good night for that."

They both got out of the car and they held hands as they walked up the sidewalk to Ann's front door.

Jimmy hugged his mom hard when she walked through the door. The dog was barking from the backyard. The house was a raised ranch, left to Ann when her mother died. Her family was local, from Lebanon, and ran the flower shop in town.

"This is Mark," Ann said to Jimmy. Jimmy stared at him. "You better show Mark how the house works."

Jimmy nodded. He held out his small hand for Mark's larger one. Jimmy's right hand had a scar on it from a hot water pipe. "Come on, I'll show you this house." He tugged Mark away from Ann and headed for the kitchen. He knelt on the floor and opened the cabinets under the kitchen sink. He held a stuffed tiger close to his chest. The pipes, silver and shiny, captured his attention. He explained to Mark about the kitchen pipes and then took him to the bathroom and explained those pipes, especially under the sink and the toilet. He took Mark down the basement stairs, pulled a string cut just the right length for him to reach. The bulb lit and he showed Mark the pipes, the boiler, and the furnace with its tiny window of fire. Mark tried to keep all of Jimmy's explanation, which rarely varied every time Mark came to the house, in his head. The way Jimmy arranged the world and then talked about it never left Mark.

That night, before Jimmy went to bed, he knelt on the floor next to his bed wearing feet pajamas with tigers on them and asked Mark to kneel next to him. The light shone in from the hallway. Jimmy started to whisper and clasped his hands. Mark couldn't make out what he was saying. Jimmy ended with amen and jumped under the covers.

"Olive juice," Jimmy said.

Mark stood up and Ann came in. She tucked Jimmy in. "Olive juice," she said.

They walked back into the living room. "What's olive juice?" Mark asked.

"Watch my lips when I say it," Ann said. She mouthed "olive juice" silently and it looked like her lips were saying "I love you." "Then you say to the person, Were you saying 'I love you'? And the other person says No, I was saying 'olive juice.'"

Water is alive and needs a house to live in. But if it lived in a house, everything would be wet, so it lives in pipes because that's polite. Hot water and cold water are friends and come together out of the faucet, to make face water, and get-the-dirt-off-Jimmy water, for a bath or big-boy shower. Water makes the suds, and hurting water comes out of the eyes, then goes down into the pipes, because water always lives in pipes. Hot water gets toasted by the furnace fire and hot water is special because it doesn't put out the furnace fire. All the water comes from a pipe under the road, the water is always moving and it goes into everybody's house, all the same. Except at Grandpa Pop's house in Vermont, he has a well, which is where water lives before it goes into pipes. Ocean water has fish in it, so it can't go into pipes because fish live in the water, that's their house, and no houses go into pipes. Almost everything is alive, and since water grows when it rains, puddles get bigger, that's how you can tell it's alive, if it grows and if it's everywhere. Water is in every house and there aren't enough numbers to count all the houses, so since water is everywhere, it's alive for sure. Looking into the furnace window and seeing the fire isn't the devil, like my dumbhead friend John said, it's the hot part of heaven, like Mom says. It speeds up your prayers and makes water hotter and gives people a little nip when they're doing the wrong thing. It helps keep them alive. Almost everything is alive. That's what my mom says. She knows about being alive and I know about tigers and being alive and water.

On Sunday, Mark drove out of Lebanon with Ann while her sister watched Jimmy. He was scouting jobs.

"I cut all those trees, on the single lot for the model," Mark said as they passed a field. The other side of the field, near a development, was still full of trees. "I should have won the bid on the rest."

"What happened?" Ann asked.

"City people. They said they wanted a bigger outfit to do it," Mark answered.

"Why?" Ann asked.

"Smaller guys don't carry enough insurance to satisfy people. Fuck them, if they think I'd drop one on their house."

"But you can understand that."

Mark gave her a bad look. "I can't afford high bond insurance," he said. His voice was lower.

Ann shrugged. "They can't afford new houses."

Slowly, Mark drove through the development and then back to town. He didn't say a word for the rest of the ride. He dropped Ann off and didn't wait for her to reach her door.

The circus came to town in the summer and so did the long-haul trucker dad. Jimmy wanted to see the circus and the long-haul trucker wanted to see Jimmy. Mark was busy cutting trees and had expanded his business to professional lawn care. He started to make better money, especially on the weekends. He was working toward weekends of the future.

Ann and Mark had coffee in Hanover, at the Coffee Blues on the corner.

"I want to take Jimmy," Ann said. "But I'm afraid Bill might, I don't know, run off with him or something." She looked across the table at Mark. "What do you think?"

"I really don't know," Mark said. "How do you get along?"

"Not well. He always had a bad temper. Look, will you come to the circus and watch us? Can you give up an afternoon of work?"

"Sure." Mark nodded. "Just sort of follow you guys around?"

"It would have to be so Jimmy didn't see you, since he knows you, but just to keep an eye on us."

"I can do that."

Ann smiled, but she seemed tired. "He'll be so intent on the tigers and what they're doing, he probably won't move much. Bill will buy him some cotton candy and feel like a dad."

"I can do that," Mark repeated.

"Okay. Get there ahead of us and stake out a good spot in the grandstand to watch us from. If something strange happens, call the cops right away and try to stop it." She shook her head. "I get worried, I mean, what if I had to go to the bathroom or something and I came out and they weren't there?"

"Let's just try to get through it," Mark said. They left the coffee shop holding hands.

The circus was set up in a farm field north of Hanover. Mark stopped work early and carefully put his tools away. He drove to the circus and went in early. Parking cost five dollars and the circus was twelve.

Ann said she wouldn't be there before six. Mark wandered through the people. He took a seat on the opposite side of the arena, like they'd agreed. He watched.

The tigers' cages were clearly visible, and soon Ann was there, looking at the tigers with Jimmy and Bill. The tigers paced back and forth on the straw in their cages. Jimmy pointed at the animals. Bill looked interested from under his ball cap. Ann caught Mark's eye a couple times and it seemed okay.

Right after the circus, Ann started taking Jimmy to a doctor in Boston and Mark wondered how she got the money from Bill to afford that. Probably he gave it to her. Money is alive, it grows and vanishes, is everywhere, all at once. Money is alive and maybe she had some money that grew. Mark never asked and she never mentioned it and Bill never traveled north again.

They were riding, scouting trees again on a Sunday. Ann watched the country go by and tried to make conversation.

"Bill's check isn't here yet."

"Maybe there'll be another circus," Mark said.

She was silent a minute. "What does that mean?" she asked evenly.

Mark shrugged.

"Well, you said it, so what does it mean?"

Mark shook his head and started to look at trees again.

"Drop me at the house," Ann said.

He watched her walk all the way to the door. She didn't look back at the truck, not once. The door opened and closed hard enough to hear it and the house seemed as unfriendly as any on the street, with the dog barking from behind it and the hedges in front. Mark felt alone as he drove away. Alone among people and places he'd known his whole life.

He never knew precisely what changed her mind. He knew he smelled like gas and oil all the time. The Friday pizza weekends didn't seem to be enough anymore. Going to Boston made her tired. It wasn't sex, they were still finding plenty of time and energy for that. But some of the things that anchor sex were missing. He'd been seeing less and less of Jimmy when Ann invited him out to dinner on a Friday night. Mark still didn't have a car, so he drove his work truck. Jimmy wasn't there.

"Where's Jimmy?" Mark asked.

"My sister's watching him," Ann said. "Mark, I've been having a hard time."

"With what?" Mark asked.

"Thinking." She paused. "I might have to move to Boston."

"What for?" Mark asked.

"I want to go to school and learn to work with people's eyes. I want to be a nurse and specialize in vision treatment."

"I can't move my business," Mark said.

"I wouldn't want you to," Ann said. "I want to get away from here for a while."

"Too many trees?" Mark tried to lighten the mood.

"Too many trees," Ann said.

Trees are alive. They're tall, they grow, they breathe air, they're everywhere. Trees have rings inside them that tell the story of how they live and the story of the world around them. A thin ring means a drought or a fire. A thick ring means a good year, lots of rain. Trees in New England farm fields sometimes have pieces of barbed wire in them, they grow around stones from old fences. These things might not kill the tree. If the tree can keep growing, can keep being alive, it can outgrow these things and bury them deep within itself. Barbed wire is not alive. Stones are everywhere, but they are not alive either.

Mark met Ann in the parking lot of her job. She was getting into her car and didn't really expect him. They hadn't spoken in two days.

"Hey, how's it going?" Mark asked.

Ann shook her head. "We should stop seeing each other."

"So that's it?" said Mark.

"Yes," Ann said.

"Are we friends?" Mark asked.

"I need some time," said Ann.

"What does that mean?"

"That means we're not dating anymore," Ann said. She pulled out of the lot and Mark watched the car moving away.

Love can die. It's a mysterious thing, the death of love. Sometimes it fades slowly, like a long sunset with amazing and rare color that lasts in the memory forever. Sometimes it becomes obese and dies from its own weight, the density and slowness that come with things grown too large. It is often killed on purpose, by someone who is in love with someone or something else. But the other person, the one still in love, is a loose end, snapping and cracking in the high wind of life passing them by. Life moves so fast it creates a back draft, that leaves things scattered and blowing in its wake. Life, of all things, is alive. It is everywhere and moves beyond speed.

Mark topped the rise and on the left sat Ann's house. Mark knew she was in Boston that day, Tuesday, with Jimmy for a scheduled doctor's visit. He pulled over to the side of the road, and then swung the whole rig into her driveway. The shepherd went nuts in the back, barking and straining at his heavy chain. Mark had half a sandwich in a bag on the front seat and took it out of the wax-paper wrapping and tossed it to the dog. He seemed to recognize Mark after that.

He started with the bushes closest to the house. He took the clippers and slowly the bushes began to resemble something. He moved to the hedge next to the road. He cut more shapes and then came some real decisions. Did he want the lawn tiger to be right if someone was looking at it from inside the house? Or from the street? From the house view, he decided. He finished and it took him three hours. Then he left.

The tree was a dancer and Mark saw that from fifty yards away. He was on a residential job in Hanover as a subcontractor, clearing a lot next to existing construction.

Whenever you cut, it isn't the wind on your face that you worry about. It's the wind seventy or eighty feet above the ground, the stuff you can't see or feel that moves and motivates what you're doing. The wind is alive and so is the sky.

The boys finished notching the trunk and cut through. The tree, rather than falling, danced on the stump. It turned, slowly, a three-quarter revolution and then began to fall, fast, forward toward the earth and the porch of the house they were working on. It hit the roof of the porch and smashed through and kept going until the earth released its invisible string and it hopped and then lay still. The owner came out and Mark got in his truck before the fireworks started.

Ann's car was in front of his house when he got home and she was sitting on the front porch.

"Hi," he said as he got out of his truck.

"Let me stop you," she said. Her voice was flat and tired but firm. "I could have had the cops over here today and you know that, so grow up. The last thing I need is you bothering me and causing problems for Jimmy." Her eyes were hard shining coal.

"I just thought—"

"This isn't about you at all, unless it has to do with you staying away from me. I'm telling you right now, I'm being friendly for the last time, right here. Next time, for anything, it's the cops." She turned and walked to her car and drove off.

Toward the end of the summer, he saw her for the last time. He pulled up to the train tracks just as the lights flashed and the gates started to go down. Right in front of his truck.

Ann and Jimmy sat in her car, waiting on the other side of the tracks, headed in the opposite direction. The lights kept flashing, the gates down. Jimmy was looking at Mark through the windshield, but neither of them made a move. Mark waited for the train. He glanced down the track in both directions. There was no whistle. He couldn't see a train.

The lights stopped flashing and the gates went up. He sat there. No train had passed. Ann sat there too and then she came across the tracks and as she got into the middle, Mark felt his whole stomach heave, because he was afraid she'd be hit. But nothing happened and she kept going, past Mark. Two cars pulled out and went around Mark before he kept on going, too.

Trains are alive. They're fast and everywhere. Trains are polite, they signal before going through town and they talk, with their loud whistle. They talk to people, warning them, and they talk to each other. Talking to each other is part of being alive.

Three years later, Mark got hurt pretty badly on the job. A branch came around and caught him, just about puncturing both of his lungs. He was in the hospital a couple of days and the bills were going to be staggering, more than he grossed in a year.

He was walking up and down the hall on his floor when he saw Ann. He knew she saw him. She was talking with a group of nurses and she moved off, toward him. She sat next to him on the blue couch.

"Mark, you look well for being in the hospital," she said.

"So do you," he said. "How's Jimmy doing?"

She smiled a bright smile. "Our little friend Jimmy is getting better," she said. "He asked about you the other day." She nodded. "Right over breakfast, he said to me, 'Where's your old friend Mark?'" She nodded again. "Jimmy says he still says your name in his prayers."

"Kids," Mark said. "That's funny. What did you tell him?"

"I said I wasn't sure exactly where you were, but I imagined you were cutting trees in the woods somewhere around New Hampshire and that you were doing fine."

"That's nice," Mark said. "I appreciate that."

"Is it true? Are you fine?" Ann asked. "Are you dating?"

Mark hesitated, then nodded. "Some days I'm better than others, like everyone." He shook his head. "But no, I'm not dating."

Ann let her head slip toward the floor. "Do you know how sad you are?"

"No," Mark said. "What do you mean?"

"How depressing the whole thing is?"

"Was it money, Ann?" Mark asked. "Did you want me to make more money?"

"I'm not going to sit here and tell you money isn't important to me and my life, but I worked as best I could and I've still got two jobs now. So no, never. Money had nothing to do with it." She paused and looked at him.

"You should tell me," Mark said. "It would help me out." A doctor and nurse walked past. "I wonder about it a lot, when I'm working."

"You're going to end up mean and alone."

Mark shrugged. "I work hard. My job isn't easy. The money's hard to earn. It drives a lot out of me."

She whispered it to him. "Because I knew in my heart Jimmy would get better," she said. "And I didn't think you would." She stood and walked out of the waiting room and into the hall and the night.

Mark sat in the darkness. His eyes hurt, but they had long forgotten how to cry. They seemed hot and dry. He opened them and they were just wet at the corners. His breathing seemed tough, like climbing a long flight of steps.

A few days later, he found himself in the hospital parking lot, under the lights, getting in his truck. He drove home. Light came out of the windows, onto the lawns, and the lawns seemed to grow onto the roads, but finally he made it home. He tried to sleep, but he couldn't. He went out again. He was next to the river, next to the train tracks.

He felt like vomiting. He wasn't going to have a family. He was working for nothing and his mean streak took over, for an instant faster than the shooting stars passing over his head in the clear black night sky. Kill yourself then, he said to himself.

He heard the whistle blow in the distance. The engine of his car was still running, the lights were still on. The driver's side door was open and the interior dome light was on. The whistle blew again, closer. There was a great roar coming down the track, and he thought for an instant that he could do it. He could stand right there and the train would do its job. Nobody would get hurt, it would be over so fast. He smelled the hot diesel fumes on the air the train pushed ahead of itself. The train ran close to its own future. Trains are alive, Mark thought. He stepped onto the track and stood between the rails, as the ground shook. The light from the lead engine flew over his head. His breath stopped then.

The whistle sounded and the train shot past Mark's car, with the steel and dark windows all moving, then gone. It wasn't until the next station that they noticed, a conductor said maybe they'd hit a deer on the tracks. The trains move so fast, how could they have known. They only knew after it was over.

The story in the paper was how Ann found out. Her sister brought it to her.

"Ann honey," she said. "There was a bad accident yesterday." Ann cried and cried until she couldn't anymore.

Bills still came to the house in Mark's name for at least a year. His brother took to writing "Deceased/Return to Sender" on them. Three or four times that winter, the phone rang with people looking for Mark to cut trees on their property. His brother answered and told them Mark had passed on and it was awkward for a minute, till they hung up. Judith Selmann called in March, looking to have the stumps on her lawn in Orford ground down. There was silence and then Mark's brother told her. Could he recommend anyone? What the hell is wrong with you, Mark's brother asked. I deliver fuel oil, I don't know anybody in the tree business except my brother. Call around and find somebody for yourself. Judith Selmann apologized for calling and sent a condolence card the next day.

A kid drowned out on the lake that year and there were some car accidents, a four-car tragedy around prom time near Deadman's Curve, and then it was the next year. Soldiers got shot and killed overseas, and their comrades shot back, killing the enemy. Hardworking local men and women lost husbands and wives and children. To diseases. Cancer was alive and enjoyed a remarkable year. A plane went down. Two planes went down. Someone lost his mind and shot up a store full of people with an automatic rifle. And then it was the next year. And then ten years later.

Time is alive, everywhere and never-stopping.

Ann looked at trees and bushes and saw shapes and animals and she knew she had done the right thing. All of life seemed like a train and we were each standing on the edge of the track at any given moment, asking if we were going to step in front of it or not.

She and her husband wanted to go visit Jimmy during his freshman year of college and she almost cried when they got to the train station in White River Junction. The rain came down heavy. A northbound train left the station as they arrived. They watched it disappear up the tracks. Her husband noticed her mood before they got out of the car.

"Are you okay?" he asked. Her husband knew most of what had happened with Mark and thought the train might bring up some memories.

"I'm okay," she said. She had never brought herself to tell her husband that she had spoken to Mark the night of his death. "It was nothing."

"You can tell me," he said.

"I wish Mark was here to know Jimmy was doing so well in school, but stupid Mark killed himself, threw himself in front of this train."

"He robbed himself of his opportunity," her husband said. "He stole his life away from himself." He put his arm around her. "It's over now. Mark wanted an ending and he got what he wanted. He made it happen."

"It shouldn't bother me to get on this train."

"I'm happy to drive you there," her husband said. "But we need to decide that now."

Ann got on the train. She and her husband managed to have a wonderful weekend with Jimmy in Manhattan.

People claim that death is not alive, yet it is ever-happening and constant. Death doesn't die. It feeds on loved ones and enemies alike and makes itself stronger and everywhere. It is insidious and comes in the form of everything. Whole nations have been killed by neighboring states on purpose and some people die by accident and every year a small city could be populated by the souls of those who chose to put themselves to death. We are here now, alive, and might be gone before morning. Death connects everything. All things that are alive have the same end. The fragility of things, the wish that a parent or spouse has to keep a child or spouse safe. The prayers, religious or not, spoken or silent. These things have their own freezing point, where they turn to ice-death. And that freezing point is only one degree away from life, and often moves faster than blessings and prayers.

The High Iron

He was on quite a run, considering summer was two months gone, and he was supposed to be a senior in high school. Not pushing his weekends out into Tuesday, not driving home drunk as the sun came up. Parked at an angle in the driveway, his two-door Buick sport coupe rested a front tire on the lawn of the raised ranch. A crushed beer can sat on the macadam. Empty liquor bottles cluttered the backseat. The fall leaves showed all bright colors in upstate New York that first week of October and soon the air would carry the echo of deer rifles.

His father woke him. "Come on, Ray," he said. He poked his head into the boy's room. "We're going out."

"What time is it?" Ray asked from his bed.

"Time to go," his father said. The beer can in the driveway and the four a.m. arrivals had bottomed out with the old man.

They got into his father's car, a gray Ford station wagon, and drove along the Hudson River toward the cement plants.

His father's friend, Bob Little Bear, worked at one of the plants as an outside night watchman. His father had got Bob a job there. Bob was waiting for them next to his watchman's shack smoking a cigarette when they pulled in.

They climbed into Bob's small motorboat. Now they were on the Hudson. The boat moved north, and Ray saw the high iron of the Rip van Winkle Bridge. They ran directly underneath it, next to one of the great stone-and-concrete bridge pilings. A kid Ray knew from high school had killed himself by jumping off. They looked over at the islands on the other side, near the eastern bank. At first Ray thought his father was looking at places to go shad fishing, although the shad were long gone. Or maybe stripers.

But his father wasn't. His father pointed across the water.

Ray saw puffs of white mist near the surface, whitecaps, and they came into focus. Albino deer. A whole herd of them, maybe a dozen, swimming through the water toward the islands. They stood up on the bank and shook themselves off. The deer were white, strangely pale, with intense red eyes.

His father pointed two fingers at the islands divided by small channels, close to shore and underneath the bridge. "That's Rogers Island, the whole thing." He talked loud, to be heard over the motor and the river.

"Who owns it?" Ray asked. "Can you fish from there?"

"I don't know who owns it," his father said. "Probably the railroad. I think you're fine, if you're in a boat."

Ray nodded.

"You couldn't shoot a deer from here," Bob Little Bear said. "The current wouldn't allow it." Ray's father nodded and cleared his throat in agreement.

"You know whales used to come up here?" his father asked. "City of Hudson was a whaling port."

"No," Ray said.

"Sturgeon, too," Bob Little Bear said.

His father looked up at the underside of the bridge. "The underside of the bridge is constructed with just as much thought as the top," he said. "People would go back to Manhattan and talk about the bridge."

Looking up at the bridge in the shifting boat brought last night's beer around in Ray's stomach and halfway up his throat. His head felt funny.

"Where do you think the albino deer come from?" Ray asked.

"Maybe," Bob Little Bear said, "they're the ghosts of people who jumped." He tossed his cigarette into the river. "No, that's speculation. It's bad to speculate like that."

They motored back to the dock in silence. On the ride home, Ray's father told him a story. The height of the bridge and seeing the cement plant made him think about it. He told it as he drove.

During World War I, Ray's father's grandfather, Bill Cooper, was hit with chlorine gas in the trenches but lived.

He came back across the ocean with a nagging cough that grew worse as upstate New York winter set in. The town doctor told him to go west, into the dry air of Arizona. He stayed and coughed until blood came up. Then he left his wife, whom he dearly loved, and ended up with a job on the Hoover Dam. He sent money home and said "I love you" at the end of every letter.

The last letter that came wasn't written by Bill. It started out "Dear Mrs. Bill Cooper." It went on to say that Bill Cooper, her husband, had died. There was some official jargon about how much money she would receive and about the death certificate. The last paragraph told the exact circumstances of his death.

Bill Cooper was working on a hanging scaffold that morning, standing suspended inside the empty shell of the dam, like all the men. The scaffold was just two wide pine boards nailed side by side, to stand on, lashed together by rope at each end, the ropes connecting to a single main rope above his head. He stood in the center, to maintain his balance, and the engineers moved him from above as he finished each section in one-hundred-and-four-degree heat, building forms for the interior concrete of the dam. His main scaffold rope broke. The planks he was standing on remained flat, horizontal, as he fell into the half-mile open middle of the unfinished dam. He fell past his boss and all the other men on their scaffolds. With his right hand, he saluted. He saluted as he became smaller, until they couldn't see him anymore. They didn't retrieve any of the men who fell. They just poured the concrete on top of them. But every man on that work crew swore that Bill Cooper saluted as he fell.

The bridge and the cement plant reminded Ray's father

of that story and he was glad to have told it to Ray when they reached their house.

In the fall now, Ray knows his duty. He drives to the cemetery and makes sure the headstones are ready for winter. He wonders which relatives left the dead flowers he respectfully puts in the trunk of his car. His phone has been disconnected for a while, and he hasn't been in touch with anyone, to know who has been visiting the graves. The tiny veterans' flags go in the trunk, too. Next spring he'll put them out again, for his father and grandfather. It can snow now, he thinks.

He stops on his way back home. He splits a ten-dollar bill between gas and two bottles of beer, which he puts under the passenger's seat, in case the cops stop him for some reason. Pulls off the road and down into the abandoned cement plant. Along the old concrete delivery road. Shuts the car off and gets out. He trespasses by the watchman's shack and out to the dock. He sees the high iron of the Rip van Winkle astride the Hudson and underneath the outline of Rogers Island.

Men are blasting in the active quarry and the boom fills the whole valley, shaking it. A train running on the eastern side headed south to Manhattan, a big silver steel snake, passes under the bridge and keeps going on the opposite shore, and for a moment the dry dead rainbow of leaves on the train track swirl up, higher, into a great cyclone pillar riding behind the train. He sees a man, as small as a boy from that distance, walking north among the apple trees on the grass bank of the train bed, above the rusted iron on cinder tracks. The dynamite in the quarry goes off again and then again, shaking the bridge, pounding his heart with the fist of God.

II

THE FUGITIVE WEST

As he was being led to jail, an enterprising reporter from the *Sedalia Dispatch* interviewed Frank James. "Why did you surrender?" the reporter buzzed. "No one knew where you were in hiding, nor could anyone find out."

Frank shot back: "What of that? I was tired of an outlaw's life. I have been hunted for twenty-one years. I have literally lived in the saddle. I have never known a day of perfect peace. It was one long, anxious, inexorable, eternal vigil. When I slept it was literally in the midst of an arsenal. If I heard dogs bark more fiercely than usual, or the feet of horses in a greater volume of sound than usual, I stood to my arms. Have you any idea of what a man must endure who leads such a life? No, you cannot. No one can unless he lives it for himself."

—Jay Robert Nash, *Bloodletters and Badmen*

The Rooming House

I was probably twelve, the August before seventh grade, tossing a baseball with my father across the front lawn that we'd just mowed together, the same as the other lawns in our circular development of raised ranch houses, a Saturday morning in upstate New York, sunny and bright, when from behind me a familiar yellow station wagon took the outside right curve of the blacktop circle too fast, bumped across the front edge of our neighbors' driveway, hit their garbage can, and kept going, faster, past us, weaving, trying to compensate, hit our mailbox—bang! straight up in the air—and turned hard left, whipping into the driveway across the street.

Fred Creight got out. He ran to the side of his house—
the strangest house on the circle, with FAY-ANN written in
white painted shingles against the black roofing shingles—
uncoiled a green hose from its hanger, and turned the water
on full blast, spraying the station wagon. He used his
thumb as a nozzle, forcing the water into a tight stream as
it drummed against the metal of the car. The windows of
the station wagon were open and he sprayed the water right
into the passenger's seat, then soaked the rear seat, too. He
dropped the hose and ran inside his house through the basement door. Every house on the circle had the same style
basement door. A solid wood door, painted white with two
centered, inset panels. A bright gold handle, and a solid,
clear glass window for the upper panel. The Creights had
hung red-and-white, vertically striped, homemade, panel-
size curtains on the inside, off a small rod screwed to the
interior of the door. The curtains moved with the air current from the door closing, stirred again, and then hung
still. The hose flipped around, snaked by the high pressure
of the water, spraying wild, spitting. Fred Creight came out
with a bucket and a sponge. He must have had some soap
in the bucket, because bubbles appeared on the car wherever he touched it with the sponge. He kept spraying the
car and soaping it up. The soap bubbles floated away, shiny
rainbow balls, over his house. He reached in through the
open tailgate window and pulled out a beer. He tilted his
head back and drained the beer, then tossed the can on his
driveway. The water pelted the car. He dropped the hose and
went back inside through his basement.

A window opened on the side of Creight's house and Fred
Creight climbed out, grabbing hold of the gutter. He pulled

on it, as if to get onto the roof, and a section of the gutter tore off in his hands. He threw it to the ground. He grabbed the roof and hoisted himself out, hanging suspended ten feet above the ground. He pulled himself up and shouted back in through the window.

"Give it here!"

A small hand gave him a boss bar, the type used for ripping shingles, five feet long, angled steel, with a sharp, pointed plate flat on the butt end. He started ripping shingles off the roof. The shingles fell onto the driveway and the station wagon, fell fast, like heavy, black snowflakes. On the roof, he attacked the word FAY-ANN. Fred Creight ripped it off with the boss bar. He pried shingles off his roof and stopped only to pull out a beer from his coat. He finished the can and threw it down to his lawn. As he bent to wrench the bar again, he slipped. He lost his footing and rolled off the roof, fell past the window he'd climbed out of, and then he was flat on his back, on the grass. When he stood, he looked right over at us and walked across his lawn and then the road and then our lawn until he stood next to us. Fred Creight was wearing shorts and a stained white T-shirt, leather hiking boots with gray socks. His short beard was dark red, same as his hair. He was a small, wiry man. I stood next to my father. Our ball gloves and the baseball lay on the fresh-cut grass.

"Hi," he said to my father.

"Hi, Fred," my father said.

"Beautiful day," Fred said.

"Yes," said my father.

"I got the mandate of heaven," Fred said.

My father nodded. "Nice."

"He spoke to me," Fred said.

"That's great," my father said.

"He said, 'Now Fred, you've done wrong this morning,'" Fred said. He looked at my father.

My father nodded. "That's private, Fred." He pointed at Fred's house. "I think you're wanted back home."

"Will you pray with me?" Fred asked. He knelt in our grass, next to my father. "It's all part of God's plan," he said. "Everything."

"No," my father said. "I won't." He paused. "Go home, Fred."

"It's the mandate of heaven," Fred said. He looked up at the sky.

"That's your business," my father said.

"Pray," Fred said. He stood. "With me." He held his hand out.

"Just go home," my father said. "You're drunk." I saw my mother watching us from the front window.

"God spoke to me," Fred said.

"No, he didn't," my father said.

"But how do you know?" Fred asked. He clasped his hands and bowed his head.

"God told me," my father said. "Get off my lawn."

Fred Creight turned around and walked back across the road, and slammed the door to his own basement as he went in. The curtains moved and with the door completely closed, the bright gold handle turned on its own, left then right, as Fred Creight locked it from the inside. His hose was still going full-bore, the water pooling in his driveway and headed for the blacktop edge of the circle. My father and I went inside through our own basement, through our door and into the cool darkness of the cinder blocks and the concrete slab floor. I put our gloves and baseball in the army duffel bag where we kept our baseball gear.

"Will that ever happen to you?" I asked my father.

My father shook his head. "No," he said. "I don't drink." He sat on the stool in front of his workbench full of tools. "Fred Creight thinks he's a giant," he said. "Drinking does that to you." He nodded. "I saw guys drink in the service. People sense that you're drunk, that you think you're bigger than you are." He balled his right fist. "That's why fights happen when you're drunk." All the hammers and planes and levels for shaping the world, for making it straight, hung on a Peg-Board over the workbench in that damp basement and he looked at me. "Drink like that and you'll end up on skid row in a rooming house, or worse," he said. Then my mother called us for lunch.

In the late afternoon, the state police were at Fred Creight's house. Drunk driving was the charge, we heard on the news. He'd hit and killed a little girl I knew in school. I passed her house, with a big front porch and gunmetal screen door, every day, from the start of seventh grade until I graduated, as I rode the school bus back and forth. Her family kept living there and I would always wonder what they did with her room, if it was still hers or not really.

Fay-Ann, Fred Creight's wife, came across the circle one day to tell my parents she was leaving, she couldn't take it anymore, the looks at the store when she shopped for groceries, the whispers, and she thanked my parents for being decent about it. The Creights moved away, and after my senior year, so did I.

*　　*　　*

But there was something before that, before high school ended. My grandfather and I went to the cemetery to tend my grandmother's grave. Maybe it was Mother's Day. We walked out through the thin trees, along the row of graves together. That was when I noticed the man standing there, three stones away from my grandmother's. I was carrying the small grass shears with black rubber on the handles.

"Hold up a minute," my grandfather whispered. He put his hand on my shoulder. He was watching the man.

"What's he doing?" I asked.

"I think he's taking a piss," my grandfather said. He coughed and cleared his throat. The man turned to face us and made a show of zipping up his pants in the process. I could smell the beer from where we stood.

"That's my oldest brother and his wife," the man said loudly. "Fuck them." Everything about him looked normal, his clothes were clean, all except his hair. It was short and dirty, sort of hacked off unevenly around his head. His chopped hair made you notice his big ears. His pants were too short and I could see his white socks.

"Hey," my grandfather said. "Don't do that shit anymore." He looked around. "These are other people's families, they shouldn't have to put up with your problems."

The man raised his middle finger to my grandfather and started across the cemetery away from us. We watched him disappear into the woods on the other side. My grandfather shook his head. "It'll catch up to him," he said.

We worked, cutting the grass around my grandmother's stone, and put a white carnation in front of it. On the way back to the car, my grandfather stopped at the stone where the man had been. "Brodell," my grandfather said. "Remember that name, Brodell." Before we reached my grandfather's huge gray Chevy, I smelled the cigars he always smoked when he drove. He wet the tip of one and lit it as soon as he sat behind the wheel. "Brodell," he said softly. "I never knew they were such drunks."

After that, long after my grandfather died, an incident happened one day with my first wife. I was drunk when people came over to visit, and as she and I stood in the driveway, our guests left and I started to wave. I waved and waved, long after the car was out of sight. Then I turned to go back in.

"You wave like a little kid," she said. "They couldn't see you. They were already gone. Kids wave like that, for too long. What's wrong with you? Why did you wave like that? Can't you see people know something is wrong with you? Do you get it or do you not get it? When are you going to stop drinking?"

I think she kept on after that for a minute as we walked back up to the house, and then I hit her. My hand was open, but I hurt her pretty bad. I can still see the dark blood rushing down her face onto her white shirt and the bubbles it made around her mouth as she breathed. Maybe I hit her again, or she fell somehow, onto the driveway. When her head hit the macadam, I think she stopped being my wife, I think that's the precise moment it occurred. To me, that is, that was the precise moment for me. I can't speak to her state of mind. But after that, we spoke to each other through court documents and cheap attorneys and I came out of the mall one day to find the word DRUNK scratched deep in the paint on the door of my truck with the sharp edge of a key.

I was headed to a bar, actually, when I noticed it, and that scratch of a word almost made me cry. Once I got to the bar, though, I felt better.

On a Wednesday night my second wife found me drunk in the living room, actually drinking and lying about drinking and she ran out of the house. She stood in the driveway, screaming at the house.

"Is this where you want to do it?" she yelled. "Is this where you hit her?" Her breathing was a loud rasp. "Are you going to come out? Come on out," she said, "let's go through the whole thing on the driveway." Her voice was so loud that it was as if she was in the living room with me. I walked over to the front window with my beer. My reflection was there, looking back at me. I looked out at my wife and grew and for a second I filled the whole house, looked out at her from every window all at once.

I followed her, hitting my head on the back door, misjudging my steps. I think she hit me first, but I ended up hitting her last and by that time, the local cops were pulling up. They broke a couple ribs on me. For an instant, my second wife and I lay on the blacktop next to each other, her from a knot on her head from me, me from the cops. Both of us ended up in the hospital that night, although I went to jail briefly after I was released. In the holding cell, I overheard two guards talking about their kids and retirement and it sounded so strange to me, to think of those things and to think it was already past me, that part of life.

*   *   *

I ended up in Seattle several years later, really just a series of rides in police cars that took me further and further across the country, in different booking rooms, from one facility to another. The place in Seattle wasn't as bad as some. One house in Ohio held mandatory group therapy and during group they made you wear shoes you picked out of paper grocery bags that sat by the front door, shoes left behind in vacant rooms by people who were long gone. At another house, everything was nailed and glued to the floor and sparks drifted to the ceiling like drunk shooting stars, out of a rusty wall-mounted heater. In Seattle, I had my own tiny room. I showered in the communal bathroom at the end of the hall and ran the cheap soap over my body and the hot water pounded my head and then I got out and toweled off with my numbered towel. On my way back down the hall, I passed one of the rooms with an open door, where this old black man, Curtis, was cutting the toe off a sock to use it as a coffee filter with a bag of coffee he'd stolen from the kitchen. I had a cup with him and found out he was the same age as me. I got dressed and went downstairs to the AA meeting because I couldn't stay at the house if I skipped a meeting. I had to have my attendance card initialed by the chairperson, and maybe there'd be a pretty girl there, like the college girl who came once and said, "Hi, I'm a new-comer," and fifty guys tried to talk to her after the meeting. All the girls looked terrible, and someone raised his hand and said everything happens for a reason, that the alcoholic, in his deluded thinking, experiences one theme, of which everything else is just a variation, and that alcoholism induces this brutal sense of urgency, a flooding of fear, over and over, like an ice ball of dread in the stomach, a freezing sharp ice ball pressing against the alcoholic's spine from the inside, and the alcoholic tries to stop this feeling, that now is the most important overwhelming moment, tries to stop the feeling with booze, and that things weren't really that urgent, everything is part of a plan . . .

I knew that was bullshit and I went upstairs and felt like I was getting bigger and walked down the hall past all the doors, all with bright gold handles and hollow, made out of leftover paneling tacked together with the cheap gold hinges screwed onto the outsides of the doorframes so when hell broke loose in one of the rooms, the house managers could just pop the hinges off and if techniques of passive restraint failed, then octagonal oak riot batons would bounce off skulls until the sodden brains held inside returned to the straight and narrow and sober.

I left and drank again and it was summer and I died every day and rode hopes of suicide through the nights and kept trying to get back to playing ball with my father, somehow. But I was back at the rooming house by winter, smaller, in a different room, as rain and snow fell across the city.

Atomic Supernova

That Monday, I drank a thermos of black coffee and was working by five a.m., just as the light started to come over the forests and high snowcaps of the Rockies. I was fixing a load of mixed metal for the three-hour haul north to Boise. I'd come out west from Ohio to work with my younger brother Tom. He owned a one-man scrap metal operation in northern Nevada—Elko County—near Jarbidge, twenty miles shy of the Idaho border. It was August and I'd been working with him about a year.

My brother and I junked and scrapped everything—cars, logging gear, old mining equipment—and managed to live off the thin, backbreaking profit. We generally trucked metal two days a week and spent the rest of the time preparing for the next job. Most loads in the scrap business are straight—I'd separate the metals with an acetylene torch and run solid batches of copper or aluminum or steel. But my brother kept a good eye on tonnage scrap prices and we were set to make an extra eight hundred dollars if we sold a heavy mixed load before Thursday. I figured this load weighed out at nine tons.

The huge blue sky was magnifying the sun. Eagles and buzzards circled on the thermal currents. Around noon, when the dead cars in the back lot were too hot to lean against, I shut down the hydraulic compactor and went for a drink of water. I walked to the front of the office, a whitewashed cinder-block building where my brother kept the books. I heard him inside, talking to somebody on the phone about a backhaul. I turned the spigot handle and let the hose run, to wash the hot rubber taste out of itself. I sat on an old plastic lawn chair, in the shade of the office. Some flies buzzed around the dog's head and he snapped at the air. I filled his metal bowl with water.

The dog heard the car approaching long before I did. We were a good mile off the connector to Interstate Ninety-three, so strangers were rare. The dog's ears came up sharp and he growled. He looked ahead, straining on his chain. I caught the signal. The mountains and the evergreens were all around, and calm, but the dog said different. The dog pulled his chain tight and looked straight down the crushed rock dirt road that led to the interstate. He was a big black-and-tan mutt, maybe part shepherd and part husky. Enough teeth and muscle to rip into business. He kept alert and so did I.

I'd had a run-in with the law back east, in Ohio. I'd been

on parole for some small-time drug sales, but I cleaned up my act. The Ohio Department of Corrections didn't see it that way, however. If I wanted to stay on the outside, they told me, I needed to sell drugs for them. A couple of parole officers were dirty, taking money, as well as five or six cops. They'd formed a little gang. I gave them ten grand a week. That went on for a while and then, they wanted more money. My partner and I had tried to make one last sale and get out.

Four of the crooked cops and two parole officers cornered us at a cheap motel after the last big sale of coke. They were going to take us in. They shot and killed my partner and in the longest, loudest heartbeat I've ever lived, it was all over. The gun was in my hand, alive, and they were all dead. It happened beyond fast—I was lucky. I didn't belong in Ohio anyway. I'd come out to Jarbidge to work with my brother and get away from that. There was more room out here. We still worked outside the law once in a while, but nothing heavy. We were going straight-edge after this last mixed load. The last bit of sketchy business would be settled, day after tomorrow. I meant it, and I think my brother did, too.

The dog growled low and I snapped my fingers. He stopped. Everything was quiet.

I heard stones crunching and finally saw a sheriff's car pulling up the long unpaved driveway. White, dirty from dust, with the Elko County star on the hood and driver's side door, and a tall antenna on the roof and two whip antennas on the trunk. The driver and another man got out. They both had silver hair and looked older. The driver wore a tan sheriff's uniform, and was smoking a cigarette. It was hard to tell just how old he was. He was a large man with a barrel chest, his silver-star badge shining in the sun.

"Hey," he said. He gave me a wave as he walked slowly toward me. I gave him a half wave back. He stopped about five feet away, reached up and took off his Stetson, wiping his brow with a blue kerchief in his left hand. He put the kerchief in his back pocket. He had a brutal-looking short-nosed revolver holstered in his duty rig, on his waist at the right side. In a natural way, his right hand never moved more than eight inches away from the butt of his gun. The safety was off. "It's a hot one," he said.

The other man stood silent. He was wearing a pressed dark blue suit, white dress shirt with a black string tie, a gray cowboy hat, and dark brown cowboy boots. He had a Colt .45 automatic holstered at his waist and his suit coat was pulled back to reveal the black raised check of the pistol's grip. His right hand rested there. His shirt was damp with sweat around the collar. From the way he held himself and the line under his coat near his left shoulder, it looked like he might be carrying another pistol in a Bianchi shoulder holster, hanging down on his left side. His eyes were red with dark circles underneath. Like he'd been crying. Both of them were giving me the hard once-over. "Hot," said the sheriff.

"It's hot where I'm standing," I said. "Blazing."

"You don't want to work much in heat like this," the sheriff said. Dust settled on the car. My brother came out of the office behind me and stood there with his arms folded. They looked him over too. I imagine they were looking for guns. Neither of us was visibly armed.

"I been ducking work for years," I said.

"Believe him when he says that." My brother nodded. He laughed, and the sheriff smiled. He raised his eyebrows at the sheriff. "Too hot for a vest?" he said. There was no bulky outline of Kevlar underneath the sheriff's tan uniform.

"What the hell's the point?" the sheriff said. He waved his left hand at the surrounding hills. "They've all got those big fifty-caliber rifles by now anyway. The vests don't stop that." He took a drag off his cigarette. "Shoot you from a mile away," he said.

"I heard that," my brother said. "Somebody told me that."

"Well, it's true," said the sheriff.

The sheriff made a motion to the silent man, who produced a small reporter's notebook and a ballpoint pen. The silent man wrote in the notebook and held it out for me to see. It read "Jim Atwell, Elko County Deputy Sheriff, Retired. I'm deaf and mute. Hello." He tipped his hat.

"He's not retarded or anything," the sheriff said. "He's just got problems." He took a hit from his cigarette. "I'm Sheriff Art Jenkins," he said. He held his hand out and we shook. "I haven't been up this way in a while." He nodded at the cinder-block office and the scrap yard behind it.

"What happened to him?" I asked. I pointed at Atwell's head.

"About thirty years ago," he said, putting his cigarette out in the dirt with the toe of his boot. "Well, the whole thing's a long story, but the main part of it is that Jim was my chief deputy at the time." He lit a new one and took a drag. He was smoking Camel nonfilters. "We had to transport a prisoner named Broughton on a governor's warrant across our jurisdiction, from Utah to California." The sheriff made an invisible east-west line in the air with his hand. "I assigned Jim to the transportation detail, as driver. So it was an escort of two officers—state troopers, big fellows—from Utah, and another deputy, Ernie Dixon from Elko County, and Jim." He motioned toward my brother. "Were you around when Ernie Dixon was around?"

My brother shook his head. "I don't recall him," he said. The dog was sitting near my brother's feet, panting.

"Before your time," the sheriff said. "Hell of a guy." He paused. "Hot to trot with the ladies, before he got married." He fussed around with his tongue inside his mouth and worked a single piece of tobacco to his lips and dry-spit it to the ground. He nodded at his patrol car. "We put those sturdy boys from Utah on either side of the prisoner and Ernie rode shotgun. Jim was driving." He took another drag off his cigarette. "Somehow, Broughton got free from the cuffs there in the backseat and grabbed a gun and shot the two Utah staties, shot Ernie Dixon in the front before Jim got his own iron loose, turned around and gave him one between the eyes." He shook his head. "I forget what Broughton had done, probably stabbed his mother and ate her or fed his kids to a dog." He chuckled. "I have no frigging idea—who knows what they do? But Jim got him and that settled Broughton's hash and I didn't see anyone crying because he's gone." He took another drag off the cigarette. "The slug went right through Broughton's head and blew the rear window out of the cruiser." The sheriff pointed at Jim Atwell. "Traumatic shock to his tympanums from all those guns going off, burst his eardrums on the spot. He was lucky to keep the car on the road." He drew the smoke into his lungs. "I guess not being able to hear, he sort of can't talk too well, either." He blew the smoke out. "He used to make noise once in a while, but he cut that out years ago."

"That's awful," I said. Jim Atwell hunched down a little,

grabbed an imaginary steering wheel with his left hand, ducked his head with a pretend horrified look on his face, made a gun with his right forefinger and thumb. He turned his upper body quickly, without letting go of the wheel, pointed the gun of his hand into the imaginary rear seat, and silently mimicked a shot and recoil with his finger. He straightened up, turned back to us, and shrugged.

"Terrible day all around," the sheriff said. "A real shit-storm." He shrugged. "The paperwork was just a mess. Broughton had killed here on Nevada soil, so we exercised legal claim over his body, but the Utah governor wanted him back for killing the troopers, even though he'd already signed him over to California, who wanted the death certificate and the body. It was a mess."

"Sounds like it," I said. "What'd you end up doing?"

"Kept him right here in a pine box," said the sheriff. "Still got him, in an unmarked grave west of here, near Golconda." He puffed his cigarette. "He shot Deputy Ernie Dixon in the line of duty, so I made sure he stayed on Nevada soil." He threw the cigarette into the dust and lit another. "I check up on him sometimes, when I'm on the road. Stop over there and take a piss right on him." He touched his fly. "It might surprise you, how often I have to piss." He paused. "I'd like to think it's motivated by hate, not age." He almost smiled. "I'm Old Testament Christian," he said, "so hate and retribution and terrible eternity"—he nodded—"that's fine by me." His right hand still stayed close to the butt of his gun. He used his left hand for his cigarette. Smoke spilled out of his mouth.

"You take care of your men," I said.

He looked up at the big sky. "Sometimes that's all you got out here," he said. "I really don't care about good and bad. I care about loyalty." He put the cigarette to his lips and inhaled and finished it. "Being a deputy is a serious thing. It affects your whole life." He shook his head. "I won't live long enough to give Jim his hearing back, so I do the best I can when I have the chance."

"Sure," I said.

He lit another cigarette with the Zippo. "Jim was my best friend," he said. "He was my best friend then and he's my best friend now. That's why we're here."

I nodded. "What can we do for you?" The dog sniffed the air.

"Well, boys, we got a bad problem," he said.

"How's that?" I said.

"Jim's son George was arrested late Saturday night."

I put my hands in my pockets. "What for?"

"That's part of it. He got arrested in Reno for passing a phony hundred-dollar bill at the craps table. He says he got the bad paper from you." He took another drag on his cigarette and his hand rested on his revolver. He pointed his thumb at Jim's suit. "We just came from talking to his boy. We got to Reno Sunday, Jim went to church and a jail visit all in the same day, in the same suit. He keeps himself neat, though, always did. I don't know how he does it." He touched Jim Atwell on the arm and Jim Atwell barely smiled. "He was Mormon for about two years after George's mother died, maybe that's got something to do with it," the sheriff said. "Now he's back to regular Lutheran." Jim Atwell watched everything without moving, primed for the draw. "Maybe we can get a look at your books," the sheriff said.

I went slowly into the office and came out nice and easy with the logbook. "Sure enough," I said. I pointed to his name

on the light blue ledger line. George Atwell. The sheriff read
over my shoulder. "He towed a car in here a couple days ago
and we scrapped it for him," I said. The total on the line indicated we'd given him two hundred fifty dollars cash for a 1977
Chevy Impala.

"Where did you get the money from, to pay him?" the
sheriff asked. "The actual bills."

"Bob Burke," my brother said. "Whole stack of hundreds
came from Bob Burke the other day."

"I've heard his name before," the sheriff said. "That's not
good."

I moved down the ledger book—the name Robert Burke
was listed next to some figures for scrapped mining equipment. Burke had paid us to haul it. On that particular day,
my brother also sold Burke two thousand rounds of ammo
and a case of blasting caps. Those items were not reflected in
the logbook. Burke, in turn, gave my brother some cash and
twenty pounds of crystal meth. My brother was supposed to
sell it to a group of bikers who were due by later in the week.
Tomorrow. Bob Burke would come by after that, to pick up
three-quarters of the cash we got from the bikers. The day
after tomorrow. It was our last piece of bad business. I'd
never actually seen Bob Burke, just hauled scrap from his
house with my brother. My brother said Burke supposedly
beat a dog to death a while ago. Nobody did anything—it
was Burke's own dog.

"Can I see one of those bills?" the sheriff asked.

I went into the safe and pulled one out. I gave it to the
sheriff and he held it out to the sun. He went back to the
patrol car and ran a special pen over it. "It's a good fake,"
he said, "but it's definitely a bad bill."

My brother kicked the dirt. "He's a cocksucker," my
brother said. He shook his head and shifted his weight from
one foot to the other.

The sheriff nodded. "Do you know where this Bob Burke
lives?" he asked.

"Up in Idaho, south of Rogerson," my brother answered.
I guess that severed our goodwill with Bob Burke.

The sheriff wrote it out on a pad to Jim Atwell, who
wrote something back to him. Then the sheriff turned to us.
"This is a little awkward," the sheriff said, and now he was
talking straight at me, "but I've got to cuff you and ask you
to sit in the back. I've actually got a warrant for your arrest
based on all this, but we'll try to straighten it out now and I
won't have to execute the warrant."

I looked at my brother. "Okay." I shrugged. I didn't have
much choice. I put my hands behind my back and he put the
bracelets on me.

"Son," the sheriff said to my brother, "check the safety on
your piece before we get too far along here, would you?"

My brother was a little surprised but obliged by pulling
his hidden Glock out of its middle-of-the-back holster and
checking it, then replacing it.

"I appreciate that," the sheriff said.

We all rode in the patrol car. Jim Atwell in the back with
me, my brother in front with Sheriff Jenkins. We pulled out
onto the connector and drove north. The road was rough and
the trees gave way to broken rocks and reddish, dusty soil.
We passed an abandoned Sinclair gas station with the green
dinosaur sign still out front.

"Do you think you can give the cigarettes a rest?" my
brother asked. "You're killing me over here." The sheriff

shook his head. "You'll get cancer," my brother said, "or give it to me and I don't want it." The smoke filled the car, even with the windows open.

"That's part of it right there," the sheriff said. "One night, maybe forty years ago or longer, Jim and me were up on a ridge drinking some beer after our shift. This was before I smoked heavy. Must have been midnight, cause we worked three to eleven. We felt a wave of heat, like the air was boiling. I'll never forget that feeling. Then bang! The whole sky lights up, everything, just like daylight for a minute, wham, the whole sky lit up and everything glowed red. Then it was gone." He dragged on his cigarette. "It was the nuclear, down south, only we didn't know it at the time. They didn't tell us." He smoked. "So I got the whole thing beat, the way I figure it. I got the chemo first, before I started smoking too much. That's the key to it, get the chemo first." He chuckled. "Jim and me, never a spot of cancer." He kept smoking. "Sheaffer, the delivery guy, he lost his hair two days later. He got sunburn all over his body, even through his clothes."

"That's a good theory," my brother said. "But you're killing me here."

The sheriff didn't seem to hear him. "That's how I learned to draw a pistol fast," the sheriff said. "After seeing that flash in the sky." He watched the road. "You have to shoot fast. It comes on like the heat and then you get that fast light. Make the air boil," he finished. He patted the big revolver on his hip. Jim Atwell wrote something on his notepad and showed it to me as if somehow he'd been listening. The note read "Man makes a lot of things go fast, but only God can make speed." Jim Atwell nodded at me and I nodded back.

We drove and passed a small ravine and a sign saying we had crossed the state line into Idaho. WELCOME. I was still cuffed in the backseat.

"Hey," my brother said. "You can't just go across the state line like that." He looked at the sheriff. Jim Atwell sat silently next to me. "You've got to notify somebody."

"It's all Elko County to me," said the sheriff. "Maybe things in Nevada grew and mutated after all the nuclear stuff, maybe the counties got bigger. Maybe the law got bigger." He puffed his cigarette. "Who do you want me to call?" he said. "Specifically?"

"I don't know," said my brother.

"Then button it," the sheriff said. "If you think normal people would ever live out here, you're fooling yourself."

We drove for forty minutes. We pulled off the interstate and snaked around, my brother giving directions, and ended up in front of Bob Burke's house. A gray cinder-block shack with concrete front steps. In the back, low cages that looked like kennels and a dog run told me Bob Burke owned dogs, which I already knew. I knew the house because I'd been there once with my brother. Two men stood near the front steps. A pickup truck idled in the front yard. A Winchester hung in the rear window of the truck. A woman sat in the front passenger's seat of the pickup truck. She didn't turn to look at us.

The sheriff stopped the cruiser and got out. He walked to the two men and I watched from the backseat. Jim Atwell and my brother watched too. "Is Bob Burke around?" the sheriff asked the two men.

One of the men scratched his chin and the other man shook his head and spoke. "No," he said. "We're looking for him."

The sheriff nodded. "We're looking for him too," he said.

He walked around to the back of the house and I couldn't see him. There was a loud crash, glass breaking. My brother got out of the cruiser and stood there, then got back in. The sheriff walked toward us from around the corner of the house. He held a couple of hundred-dollar bills in his hand. He put the bills on the dashboard of the cruiser. They looked real. I was cuffed in the backseat, sweating. Jim Atwell sat next to me, in his own silent world. He was sweating too.

The sheriff walked to the pickup truck, to the passenger's side next to the woman. He spoke to her softly. The two men came over and stood with him and the men and the sheriff walked to the back end of the truck.

One of the men spoke up. "If we didn't find him here, we were going to go over to The Fifth Ace and see if he was there. He drinks over there sometimes."

"Regular," the other man said. "I see him there every day when I drive past, with his big yellow truck parked out front." The hot sun was moving a little over the Rockies.

"How come there's two of you?" the sheriff said.

"Burkey's pretty mean," the one guy said.

"Burkey's fast with a gun," the other man said. "He thinks I'm afraid of him, but I'm not." He looked up at the sky and then at the sheriff. "I'm not," he said.

"Sure you're not," the sheriff said.

"That's my wife," said the man, pointing at the woman in the front seat.

"How long you been married?" asked the sheriff.

"We're not yet, but we're going to be soon," the man said. "We're supposed to get married."

"That's nice," the sheriff said.

"Nobody hits my wife," the man said. "Did you see her? Bob Burke did that to her."

"I saw her," the sheriff said.

"She might be pregnant," the man said. "We might lose our baby."

"Where was she when Burke hit her?" the sheriff asked.

"She was at The Fifth Ace, having a beer, minding her own business," the man said.

"Where were you?" the sheriff asked.

"I was in Spokane for a couple days and I come home to this," the man said.

"We're going," the other man said.

"I'll follow you to The Fifth Ace," the sheriff said. The two men pulled out onto the highway in their pickup and we followed right behind. After fifteen minutes, we turned into a run-down strip mall, set off the road by a big parking lot. The lot held about ten cars, baking in the sun. As we parked in the back, Jim Atwell wrote a note on his pad and handed it to the sheriff. I didn't see what Jim wrote, but the sheriff's reply read "Dog dead in kennel—woman beat bad—eye socket maybe broke." The two men parked their truck so all I could see of the woman was the back of her head and her dirty blond hair. From the way her head moved, it looked as if she was smoking cigarettes constantly.

We sat there and waited. At least I did—the rest of them got out of the car. The sheriff, Jim Atwell, my brother, and the two men stood on the concrete sidewalk, watching the parking lot from the shade of the overhang. We had pulled into a corner of the lot and the cruiser was hidden behind the deserted store. At the other end of the strip mall was The Fifth Ace, then a Laundromat, then another deserted

storefront, then the store we were next to. In front of the
store was a kid's coin horse. MISTER QUICKLY was written
on the bottom of it, on the rectangular base. Jim Atwell patted Mister Quickly on the head. The men stood, waiting in
the heat.

A kid, a young boy, came out of the Laundromat. He
walked down by us. I sat cuffed in the back of the cruiser.
The sheriff tossed his cigarette in the parking lot as soon as
he saw the kid.

"Hi," said the kid. He had on little jeans, black sneakers,
and a white T-shirt, and a short, done-at-home haircut. He
picked at a small scab on his right forearm. His belt buckle
was an oversize fake gold baseball.

"Hi there partner," said the sheriff. The other men looked
at the kid.

"I'm Stevie," the boy said. He adjusted his pants.

"Hi Stevie," the sheriff said. "I'm Sheriff Jenkins."

"I'm five," Stevie said.

"That's great," the sheriff said. He didn't take his eyes off
the parking lot. Jim Atwell looked at Stevie and then back
at the parking lot. His right arm was a coiled spring, ready
to draw that big .45. I tried to imagine what firing a gun and
not hearing the shot would be like.

"How many old are you?" Stevie asked.

The sheriff looked down at him. "I'm eighty-seven," said
the sheriff. It didn't seem to register on Stevie. A truck
pulled into the parking lot, but it wasn't Bob Burke.

"I'm going to ride this horse," Stevie announced. The
horse was directly behind the men.

"For Christ's sake," said my brother.

"Oh, put a quarter in," one of the men said.

"Fuck you," my brother said. "You put a quarter in."

"Come on," said the sheriff. "Don't curse in front of the kid." He looked back at the parking lot. Jim Atwell stared at the heat devils coming off the black macadam and the cars.

"Yeah," Stevie said. "No cursing."

My brother shook his head. The two other men laughed.

"My mother doesn't like cursing," Stevie said.

"I bet I know what your mother likes," my brother said.

"What?" Stevie said. The sheriff looked at my brother.

"Never mind," said my brother. "You want to ride the horse, fine." He put a quarter in for the kid and lifted him up into the saddle. Nothing happened. A car pulled into the lot and an old woman got out and headed into The Fifth Ace.

"He's not going," Stevie said. "Make him go."

My brother put another quarter in the silver slot. Nothing happened. "You know what they do to horses that won't go?" my brother asked. Stevie shook his head and in an instant, my brother was holding his Glock up to Mister Quickly's cast-iron brown ear. "They shoot them," my brother said. "Bang." The color drained out of Stevie's five-year-old face. My brother put the Glock away.

The sheriff turned around. He pointed his chin at the two other men. "Make it go for the kid," he said. "Pick it up."

The two men strained at either end of the horse, shifting it around a little.

"Giddyup," Stevie said.

The man at the head of Mister Quickly said, "I got the good end." He laughed.

They shifted the horse around and Stevie whooped it

up. The painted expression on Mister Quickly's face never changed. He kept charging ahead at the same rate. Even though Mister Quickly was a racehorse, a tan thoroughbred, there was a painted-on rifle in his saddle scabbard.

The sheriff went to the car and reached up on the dashboard. "I've got something for you, Stevie," he said. He came out holding a tin star. He knelt and pinned the star on the kid. "You're a deputy now," the sheriff said. A pickup truck pulled into the parking lot and turned around, headed back out onto the highway.

"Wow," Stevie said.

"Do right by the law and the law will do right by you," the sheriff said. "Look out for bad guys." Jim Atwell stood at attention and saluted.

"What should I do if I see one?" Stevie asked.

"What do you think you should do?" the sheriff asked.

Stevie looked at my brother for a moment, then back at the sheriff. He made a pistol with his thumb and forefinger. "I know what to do," he said.

"That's right," said the sheriff.

"Are you the good guy?" Stevie asked.

"I'm the only guy," the sheriff said.

Stevie turned around and walked on his little legs toward the Laundromat. He turned around and saluted before he went inside. My brother made a noise.

"Don't be such an asshole," the sheriff said. He lit a cigarette.

"I don't like kids," my brother said. A truck went by on the highway.

"Nobody does," the sheriff said, "but what the fuck does that have to do with anything?" He spit. "Jim's the only one here who cares about kids." He took a drag on his cigarette. "You're a grown man. Keep your act together, before we have a problem."

"Right," my brother said.

"No, seriously, son," the sheriff said. "Keep that shit in mind." He nodded. He watched the parking lot hard. Somebody pulled into the parking lot in a big yellow four-by-four. A man got out.

"That's not Bob Burke," one of the two men said.

"But it looks like his truck," the other man said. He squinted in the sun. "It's not him though," he said. "Burkey's bigger than that."

The sheriff stuck two fingers in his mouth and whistled loud. The man who was driving Bob Burke's truck turned to look, and the sheriff motioned him over. He walked across the parking lot. He had a cowboy hat on, with jeans and a black T-shirt.

"Hi," said the sheriff. "Is that Bob Burke's truck you're driving?"

The man slowed and nodded. "Yes it is," he said. Half a tattoo showed from under his sleeve on his left biceps.

"Burke around?" the sheriff asked. I saw the man's eyes take in the size of the sheriff's gun.

"No," the man said. He paused. "I'm no friend of his," he said. "Just doing him a favor to get some money he owes me." He nodded. "Legal."

"When's he back in town?" the sheriff asked. He lit a new cigarette.

"Day after tomorrow," the man said. Jim Atwell stood, watching. He was looking right through the man.

"Fine," the sheriff said. "You never saw me and I never

saw you and you get your legal money and that's all you know." He took a long drag.

"You're a stranger that just became a ghost," the man said, "as far as I'm concerned." He started to walk away, toward The Fifth Ace.

"Because I'll come back," said the sheriff. He puffed his cigarette.

"Burke's not my friend," the man called over his shoulder. "You can have him." He kept walking. He went into The Fifth Ace.

The sheriff and my brother and Jim Atwell got into the cruiser. As we pulled out of the parking lot, I got a clear view of the woman's face in the pickup truck. I've never seen those colors of deep purple and blue-black. She didn't look at us.

We drove back across the Idaho state line, into Nevada. We turned off the connector, onto the dirt road of the scrap yard, and stopped, a mile from the scrap yard. The sheriff and Jim Atwell got out of the car and exchanged notes on Jim's notepad. My brother got out of the car. I was still sitting cuffed in the rear seat.

"What's that you're wearing?" my brother asked. He nodded at the sheriff's pistol.

"Smith and Wesson six twenty-nine-V, forty-four Mag," the sheriff said. Jim Atwell walked around the cruiser and got in the passenger's seat. He took his hat off and nodded at me. I nodded back.

"It looks like a real stopper," my brother said.

"Oh this is a widow-maker from way back," the sheriff said. "This thing will shoot to China." It was in his hand, more quickly than was possible.

"You're a fast draw," my brother said. "Some guys draw fast and it's a trick, but it looks like you could shoot that way."

"You can talk about all the fancy trick shooting you want, but unless you can grab it and hit the other guy before he hits you, it's all talk." He reached down, put the gun in his duty rig, and before I could breathe, he drew it again. "You can't beat me," he said to my brother.

"No," my brother said, "I probably can't."

"No probably about it," the sheriff said. He tossed his cigarette into the dirt road. He holstered the ugly Magnum.

"But that doesn't matter," my brother said.

"Not today it doesn't," the sheriff said.

"I've got good friends in the hills," my brother said. "Friends that don't care about shit."

The sheriff patted his Magnum. "Like Bob Burke? He was your friend yesterday. And then today he's got you involved with phony money and he beat someone else's wife and it looked like he crippled a dog or two, maybe killed one." He paused. "Someday the shit he won't care about will be you. How do you know he's not coming here to kill you? You think he's steady?" He shook his head.

"I guess I don't," my brother said.

The sheriff patted his Magnum again. "I've got six good fast friends right here," he said. "My friends are like Jim Atwell. Steady." He nodded at me in the car. "I heard you draw pretty fast."

"No," I said. "Not me. I'm afraid of guns."

"That's not what I heard," the sheriff said. "I heard you're fast."

"Who'd you hear that from?" I said, sweating. Jim Atwell looked at me from the front seat. I felt like I could hear his silence.

"I got it on pretty good authority that you shot four Ohio cops before they even got their guns out." He paused to light a cigarette. "They tried to tell me you shot your partner and got away."

"Never happened," I said. With my eyes, I told my brother to stay cool.

"That's what I said too, till they faxed me the report." He puffed his cigarette. "They forgot to mention the two parole officers that got killed. Some Ohio detective who claimed to be working the cold case squad called a month ago. They had you surrounded in that motel, three squad cars, two officers in each car, pulled right up front and went to get out and you came out of that front door and shot those men to death fast like nobody's business and turned around and shot your partner so he wouldn't squeal. Didn't make sense to me." He looked up at the sky. "They only got one shot off, six trained officers. A couple of them didn't even clear leather with their piece. That's what the forensic report said." He looked over at me. "Now that's fast," he finished.

"I don't know what you're talking about," I said.

He waited a minute. "Well, I didn't say anything to him." He took a hit off his cigarette. "He talked to me like I was a hayseed, so I didn't say anything to him. I told him we didn't have anybody like that out here in Elko County and if a man could really draw that fast, I'd make him my deputy." He nodded at me again. "That would be a good idea, wouldn't it?"

"That'd be a good idea," I agreed. "What about cops sticking together?"

"That shit ends at the Mississippi," he said. "I don't tolerate dirty cops. If it was a regular takedown, why was parole involved? It smells like a bad operation gone worse."

He took his hat off and wiped the sweat from his brow with his red kerchief. "You probably don't know this, but right over there somewhere was the last stagecoach robbery in the U.S. in nineteen sixteen." He pointed into the woods.

"Really," I said.

"Yup," he said. "Outlaw named Judson robbed a mining payroll coming down from Rogerson to Jarbidge in the middle of a December blizzard. He shot four or five road agents they'd hired as guards, but one of them winged him. They caught him by the blood trail."

"Hmm," I said.

"But the governor pardoned him, and when he got out he hung around for a bit and then disappeared, with the money he'd hidden. I kind of like that story."

"It's a good story," I said.

"When I was a kid, I used to tell people that my grandfather had changed his name from Judson to Jenkins."

"Did he?" I asked.

"Not likely," he said. "Come here, get out of the car." He opened the back door and helped me out. He unlocked the cuffs. I rubbed my wrists. Jim Atwell leaned over and handed him something through the open driver's side window. "Are you ready?" he said.

"Yes," I said. "I'm ready."

He pinned the star Atwell had handed him on my blue denim work shirt. "By the power vested in me by the state of Nevada, I hereby make you a full deputy of the Elko County Sheriff's Department." We shook hands. I felt the weight of the star on my shirt.

"Thanks," I said.

"Now we're going back to Reno"—he jerked his thumb

at Jim Atwell in the cruiser—"and arrange for his son to get out of lockup. I think I can arrange that on the basis of our ongoing investigation into Bob Burke."

"Sure," I said. "That sounds good."

"And Bob Burke will be back here the day after tomorrow," he said.

I nodded. My brother spoke up. "That's right," my brother said.

"Well, I'm going to be here, too," the sheriff said. "I might have to shoot Bob Burke." The Magnum was in his hand and he spun it once around on his forefinger and jammed it back in its holster. "I can feel it coming on," he said.

"I'm with you," I said.

"If I'm not here, you might have to shoot Bob Burke," he said. "We're doing this for Jim and Jim's boy. Remember that."

"I know," I said.

"How fast are you?" he asked.

I had the star on now. "Faster than you've ever seen," I said.

"Now you're talking," the sheriff said. "Strap on an iron and let's see it."

My brother took off his belt and gave me the small holster he'd been using to hold his Glock. I put it around my waist. My arm felt good and my wrists had recovered from the cuffs. The gun was in my hand.

"Let me see that again," the sheriff said.

I put the Glock back into the holster. I shrugged and the gun was in my hand.

The sheriff shook his head. "Oh," he said, "that's some kind of fast."

"Thanks," I said. "I won't let you down." I looked inside the cruiser at Jim Atwell.

The sheriff climbed in behind the wheel and lit a cigarette. "If I'm not here day after tomorrow," he said, "you go ahead and kill Bob Burke and we'll figure it all out later."

"Okay," I said.

"You're going to like it out here in the West," he said.

"I like it already," I said.

The sheriff pulled away and my brother and I stood at the end of our dirt driveway. We walked up into the woods a little, talking about what had happened and trying to imagine the precise spot of that last stagecoach robbery and the gunfight in the December blizzard of 1916. We talked about catching some bull trout. We talked about the mystery of how God makes speed.

Then we walked back to the scrap yard and waited for Bob Burke to show.

The Copper Kings

After my wife divorced me last August, I left upstate New York and drove west. I think I had a plan about living in Seattle, but no cash to make it happen. I got stuck in Moscow, Idaho. I devoted a lot of time and attention to heavy drinking and found I was really good at being drunk.

Functional alcoholism requires a delicate balance of solitude, booze, and money, and I worked on making a science of it. Keeping the money part of the equation flowing is always tough, so I was relieved when Greg showed up on my doorstep early one Saturday morning, talking about getting paid cash for a day's work.

Greg was a big ex-football player who lived with his girlfriend and her son in one of the trailers that surrounded my one-bedroom, cinder-block shed. Greg sold insurance, and he painted houses, but his main sideline was bounty hunting and skip tracing. He was licensed by the state of Idaho as a guide, so most of the things he did were somewhere in the neighborhood of legal. In Idaho, you can drink a beer in your car with a pistol right on the front seat. I don't think they let things like licenses get in the way of things like justice, so Greg and I could probably hunt down anyone we could find. If you went after somebody, you had to know they had the same access to fast lead and self-protection that you did. God didn't make men equal; Sam Colt did, the saying goes, and Idaho respects that. Every time I saw Greg outside his girlfriend's trailer, I waved and he waved back. We were partners, in an unofficial sort of way. I saw him walking up the gravel road that wound through the trailers, and I opened the door before he knocked.

"Hi," I said. Greg wore a denim shirt, jeans, a tan hunting vest, and black cowboy boots.

"Early to be stinko, isn't it?" he asked, pointing at the beer in my right hand.

"That's a myth," I answered. "Alcohol doesn't even begin to affect your brain before noon."

"Sure," Greg said. He nodded. "Feel like taking a ride? I've got a potential client and we could get paid cash for working today."

"How much?" I asked.

Greg shifted his weight and looked out over the trailers. "I think that depends," he said.

"Ballpark it for me." I leaned against the doorjamb and sipped my warm beer.

"It's a missing person job," he said. He turned to look straight at me. "Could be a couple hundred bucks in it, and probably no guns." He paused. "Well, maybe guns, but definitely no cops."

I nodded. "I'm in," I said. I tilted my head and drained my beer, tossing the empty can back into my apartment. "Can I use your pistol?" Greg owned a Beretta that I coveted.

Greg smiled. "Sure. Let's drive over."

We walked back down the gravel road together and got into Greg's ugly truck, an old Toyota four-door that he'd rigged with a Plexiglas barrier, separating the front seats from the back, just like the cops. He started it up and we drove across town and out into farm country. Mile after mile of lentils and corn stretched to the horizon.

"Nice country," I said. A bottle of whiskey sat in my jacket pocket. I took it out and had a swallow. I looked at the fields passing by.

Greg leaned over, reached into the glove compartment, and handed me the Beretta. I stuck it in the right-hand pocket of my work jacket.

"Farms always scare me," Greg said. "Too much work." He watched the road straight ahead, oceans of grain passing on both sides. "I like a town," he said. "No matter how small a town."

We passed a long-abandoned church and made a right turn onto a dirt driveway. A hand-lettered sign read RYAN'S FARM. I sucked back some whiskey. We drove down the dirt driveway and stopped in front of a white house surrounded by farm buildings. A sagging picnic table sat on the front lawn. An old man walked off the porch toward us. An older, white-haired woman stood on the porch steps, in front of the house. We both got out of the truck and I left the whiskey under the passenger's seat.

"Hi," said the old man. His voice was a ton of gravel coming off a truck. "I'm Harry Ryan." He wore farmer's denim coveralls and a green ball cap.

Greg nodded. "I'm Greg Newell and this is my partner, John Thorn," he said. I nodded and lifted my right hand in a half wave.

"Sam Haag said you were a good man for this job. Sam said you were tough." Harry Ryan looked at Greg, then at me. "I need somebody tough," he said.

"We're tough," Greg said.

Harry Ryan came closer. "I smell booze," he said.

"I spilled some on my boots last night, out playing pool," I lied.

Harry Ryan came a step closer. "Smells like you spilled it in your mouth first thing this morning," he said.

"It helps me be tough," I said.

Harry Ryan nodded.

"His wife divorced him," Greg said.

Harry Ryan put his hands in his pockets. "I understand," he said. He walked over to the picnic table and sat down. Greg and I followed and stood on the other side of the table. Harry Ryan looked up at us.

"Well," he said, "I want you to find my son." He held out an envelope. "He went up into the Panhandle to get a job and sent us some letters, like this one. But the letters stopped three weeks ago and I haven't heard from him." He handed the envelope to Greg, and Greg opened it, taking the letter

out. He held it over near me, so I could read it too. It was
written in a bad scrawl.

*Dad—here's nine hundred dollars and more is coming. Every-
thing is fine. I'm working up north, mining, working for the copper
kings and the pay is good. I'm working hard and will see you and
Mom soon. Love, Mike.*

"I want you to find him," Harry Ryan said. "If you find
him, I'll give you five hundred dollars." The white-haired
woman slowly turned and walked up the porch steps, back
into the farmhouse. The screen door closed with a smack
against its wood frame. Harry Ryan went on, quietly. "Mike
was in some kind of small trouble in Boise that I didn't even
know about. Some probation officer and a state cop stopped
by here yesterday, but they wouldn't tell me anything. Just
said they were looking for Mike." Harry Ryan put a photo-
graph on the picnic table. "That's Mike," he said. The picture showed a smiling young man next to a brand-new
pickup truck. In the back of the truck stood a Doberman.
Greg picked up the picture.

"Is that his dog?" Greg asked.

"That's Max," Harry said. "Mike trained him and never
went anywhere without him."

"Was Max a vicious dog?" Greg asked.

Harry smiled. "He'd take your leg off. Max was better
than a gun, as far as I was concerned." He looked up into the
giant blue sky and then out over the fields. Then he stood
and handed Greg some money. "That's two hundred fifty.
You get the rest when the job is done." Harry Ryan started
to walk back to his house.

"Fine," Greg said. He nodded his head once. Affirmative.
I did the same. He cleared his throat and kept talking.

"That's fine." He handed me the picture and we both got into the truck. Harry Ryan never turned around, just walked up the porch steps and into the farmhouse. I took a slug of whiskey and watched the same fields roll by.

We drove back to town and Greg pulled over at a phone booth outside a gas station. I watched him making call after call, laughing and shaking his head in the little booth. Then he came back to the truck.

"Who'd you call?" I asked.

Greg looked at me and narrowed his eyes. "It pays to cultivate reliable underworld contacts," he said.

"Who'd you call?" I asked.

"Smitty and my ex-girlfriend," he said. Smitty was an old biker friend of Greg's who owned a bar just outside Bonners Ferry, way up north in the Panhandle. I didn't know the ex-girlfriend. "Smitty says he knows a reopened copper mine in the hills, might be just what we want. He's going to ask around and get us directions. But we need cover."

"What?" I said.

"Cover," Greg said. "A disguise, so we can get in the place." Greg turned around in the gas station parking lot and doubled back into town. He pulled off into a side street and stopped in front of a red house. "Just a minute," he said. A woman came out onto the front porch and from the excited way she looked at Greg, she appeared ready to move off the ex-girlfriend list, back into the active rotation. She and Greg went inside and I had a couple shots of booze. I wished for a cup of coffee to kind of even me out, but all I had was whiskey. So I took two more swallows, just to stay steady and tough.

The minute turned out to be three-quarters of an hour,

and finally, Greg came back down the front steps. Walking next to him was the biggest dog I've ever seen on a leash. The dog was black and tan, about the size of a small pony. He let the dog in the backseat and the whole truck rocked. Greg got in and started to drive.

"What the hell's that?" I asked.

"Mister Lucky," Greg said. "He's our cover. He'll get us in." Mister Lucky's head slammed into the Plexiglas barrier as we hit a pothole. He didn't even seem to notice it. His head was bigger than a basketball.

"What breed is he?" I asked.

"Neapolitan mastiff," Greg said. "Real killers." Mister Lucky lay down across the backseat. He looked cramped and slightly mad.

"How much does he weigh?" I asked.

"I don't know," said Greg. "Maybe two thirty, two forty. A real killer."

We drove north toward Bonners Ferry. I looked out the window the whole way, but I didn't see anyone who looked like Mike Ryan. The Rockies were on our right and they seemed to grow as we headed north.

We stopped at Smitty's. Two motorcycles and a pickup truck rested outside in the dirt parking lot. Greg got out, and I followed him inside. A dark bar, with a jukebox, a pool table, and not much else. Mounted over the bar was a full-size log, split down the middle. Somebody had used a wood-burning kit to carve the words IN GOD WE TRUST AND YOU AIN'T GOD. Three or four regulars inside. They must have been regulars, because even the most simpleminded folk wouldn't just wander into Smitty's. For all of the country up in the Idaho Panhandle, nobody wandered. It was all very deliberate. There were places you weren't supposed to go, sort of a widely held secret. We were headed for one of those places. Smitty talked in a low voice with Greg, gave me a half wave, and then we walked back out to the truck. Mister Lucky didn't move.

"Did Smitty help out?" I asked.

"Sure," Greg said. "Here's where you earn the money." He took another pistol, a .45 Colt Combat Commander, out of the glove compartment and slid it under his left leg. "Just in case," he said. I reached into my jacket pocket and clicked the safety off the Beretta. I took my last slug of booze and put the bottle on the floor. We were ready.

Greg drove up into the mountains for forty minutes, following winding roads, passing logging sites and skidder tracks that headed straight into the woods. My ears popped as we went up. Eventually, we drove up about a mile of dirt road.

"I think this is it," Greg said.

Ahead of us stood an iron gate and a small shack with a small sign that read COPPER KINGS MINING. A man sat on the gate, his rifle propped up against the shack. We pulled up. The man got off the gate and walked over to the shack. He called to us as he picked up the rifle.

"Mine's closed for the day, boys," he said. He walked toward us, cradling the rifle in his arms. "Mine's closed and we aren't hiring." He looked into the truck at Mister Lucky, who stood up and looked back. "Nice pup," he said.

Greg leaned out his truck window and held up two twenties. "Look at that," he said. "These are some of those new

twenties." He looked closely at the bills. "Much bigger picture of Jackson," he said.

The man who was pretending to be a legitimate guard
came over. He took the two twenties out of Greg's hand.

Greg nodded. "Aren't those new bills?" Greg asked.

"It's hard to tell in this light," the man who was a guard
said.

"Well, you keep them for me and find out," Greg said. "I
understand you might have to spend them to do it, but you
be sure to find out." He gave the man who was a guard but
didn't want us to think he was a guard a friendly fake smile.
The man gave the same smile back to him. The man walked
over to the shack and the gate went up. Greg pulled up.

"Go on in and tell Charlie you've got a dog on for tonight,"
the man who was guarding something that wasn't a copper
mine said.

"How will I know it's Charlie?" Greg asked.

"He's the biggest biker you've ever seen," the man said.
"And he's got the biggest gun you've ever seen too." Then
he waved us through.

Greg drove in. We passed some abandoned mining
buildings, some industrial equipment and covered convey-
ors. A couple of pickup trucks were parked next to the buildings. No mining going on here.

"Smell that?" Greg asked. I nodded. It was a strange mix-
ture of gasoline and ether. "Copper mine my ass," Greg said.
"This is the biggest crystal meth plant in the world." I
reached down, got the whiskey bottle, and took a sip. Ahead
of us swarmed a lazy crowd of men, lounging around on the
tailgates of pickup trucks, talking and drinking beer. Each of
them had some type of dog, ranging from German shepherds

to huskies. Once in a while, a dog barked. A huge biker—
Charlie I assumed—sat behind a table in front of an entrance
to a mine shaft. We heard the small roar of a crowd coming
from inside the shaft, along with the sounds of the dogs.
Greg parked the truck and got out with Mister Lucky on the
leash. "You take the gun," he said quietly. We walked up to
the table. Mister Lucky dwarfed all the other dogs we saw.
We stepped up to Charlie.

"You want to fight that dog tonight?" Charlie asked. He
was huge, even sitting down. He must have weighed over
four hundred and fifty pounds. On the table in front of him
sat the wickedest-looking gun I'd ever seen. It was a nickel-
plated shotgun, short-barreled, but with a cylindrical mag-
azine at the butt end. Charlie noticed my gaze. "That's a
Streetsweeper. Nineteen shots as fast as I can pull the trigger,
one in the chamber, eighteen in the clip." He looked at me.
"Evens things up pretty fast, know what I mean?"

"I know what you mean," I answered.

He turned back to Greg and Mister Lucky. "So how about
it?" he said.

Greg shook his head. "No," he said. "We just used him
to get through the gate."

Charlie's face did something that it probably considered
a smile. "Got to get better help around here." He shrugged
and looked up at Greg. "If you're a cop, this is your grave."

"Do I look like a cop?" Greg said.

Charlie shrugged. "They look different nowadays," he
said. "Used to be easy—anyone with shiny shoes and a short
haircut. But now . . ." He paused. "Well, it's not so easy."

"Sure," Greg allowed. "I'm just looking for somebody."
He took the picture of Mike Ryan out and put it on the table

in front of Charlie. The terrible sounds of dogs fighting came from inside the mine shaft, echoing out over the buildings. "Ever seen him?" Greg asked.

Charlie was quiet and then he coughed. "That kid's gone," he said. "Forever."

"How did it happen?" Greg asked.

"He stopped breathing, that's how it happened. Like it always happens." He looked at Greg. "Pure accident," he said. "Lots of accidents in this life."

"Right," Greg said. Lightning moved slower than Greg in that next instant, and I was the thunder only a second behind. He had Charlie down on the ground, his right foot on Charlie's throat and Mister Lucky's mouth less than an inch from Charlie's right eye. I had the Streetsweeper, safety off, and was keeping an eye on the men behind us. "Whisper it to me," Greg said to Charlie. "Tell me about the accident. And don't do anything to disturb the dog. He's edgy." A low growl, like a distant airplane engine, was coming from Mister Lucky's throat.

"The kid was on probation in Boise," Charlie whispered. "He worked up here for three weeks, transporting meth and winning with his dog. Then we caught him wearing a wire." Charlie's breathing was shallow. Greg increased the pressure of his foot. Charlie croaked it out. "We put him in with the dogs."

Greg took his foot off. Mister Lucky stayed ready until Greg tugged on the leash. The crowd of men behind us was quiet. Charlie got up slowly.

"No hard feelings," Greg said. "I had to know."

Charlie rubbed his Adam's apple. "Your nights are going to be very dark and scary," he said. He gave Greg a hard stare. I turned around with the Streetsweeper and my tough kicked in.

"You drugged-out freak!" I shouted. "I've got ten of my buddies, all saw action in Somalia, within an hour of here, you want me to call in a hailstorm from hell?" I was shaking inside, the Streetsweeper less than an inch from Charlie's nose. "They'll feed you your own ass," I said. "You want some?" I stared at him. "Do you want some!" The trigger pressed back against my finger and the whiskey tough wanted to squeeze it.

Charlie shook his head. He watched us as we walked back to the truck and pulled away. We waved to the man at the gate as we passed through. He'd probably be dead by morning for letting us in. He waved back. I pointed the business end of the Streetsweeper at the floorboard of the Toyota, ready to be dangerous if I had to be. Mister Lucky owned that backseat.

The sun started to set as we drove back to Moscow and we rode through a hard, fast rain that blew through and then broke into sun again. Greg cleared his throat as we reached the outskirts of town.

"Do you have buddies that fought in Somalia?" he asked.

"No," I said.

"Even fooled me."

We pulled into Harry Ryan's driveway and Harry Ryan came out of the farmhouse. We unloaded ourselves from the truck and I left the heavy-duty shotgun on the passenger's seat. The white-haired woman was sitting on the porch steps. Harry, Greg, and I walked over by the lentil field. It

seemed to stretch out forever. Harry had his back to us, looking at the field.

"How's my boy?" he said. "Did you find him?"

Greg looked at the ground and then at Harry Ryan's
back. "He's working," Greg said.

As soon as Greg spoke, Harry Ryan started to gently cry.

"He's working up north for the Copper Kings, just like
he wrote you," Greg said.

Harry Ryan nodded. "Lie to me again," he said. I could
hear him crying as he spoke. "Lie to me, tell me the best one
you've got." He was sobbing. "The money's on the picnic
table," he said, turning to walk toward his farmhouse. When
I looked, the old woman on the porch was gone. I wondered
if this was the hardest day of her life. Probably not. The
Ryans didn't seem like folks who got good news very often.
And they didn't have the luxury of collapsing too hard,
because they needed to be working the next morning.

I picked up the money as we walked back to Greg's ugly
truck, and we drove away.

Underdogs

Like I said, my plan was to hole up in Seattle, but my traveling money wore thin before I made it. I took a job as a fence cutter on a three-hundred-acre farm outside Moscow, Idaho. The country out there was just mile after mile of grain and lentil fields, against the background of the Rocky Mountains. The hard work suited me fine—I'd worked construction back east and was handy with a chain saw. I rented a one-bedroom, cinder-block apartment next to some trailers on the north edge of town and settled into the lifestyle of a functional alcoholic. I drove out to the farm early every morning, worked all day, and bought my whiskey and beer from the package store on the ride home. In the space of two weeks, I was giving a neighborly wave to recognizable trailer tenants and making sure I didn't hit their children with my pickup truck when I pulled in front of my apartment in the late afternoon. And although I'm no saint, I passed on a midnight offer of drunken sex from one of the semimarried women who always seemed to be out on their trailer porches, sitting, waiting for something. Life had lost a lot of its shine at that point and I didn't think encounters with angry husbands or boyfriends would be the right way to polish things back up.

I'd been there about a month when somebody knocked on my door around lunchtime on a Saturday. I opened the door and it was Greg.

"Busy?" he asked. His voice was deep.

"No, not really," I said. "Come on in." He stepped over the empty cases of beer and sat on my ratty couch. I fell into the chair across from him, sipping my beer. The once-blue fabric on the chair was so threadbare that the wood frame showed through. "Want a beer?" I asked.

"No," he said. He looked at his watch. "I got a proposition for you and I need a fast answer."

"Go ahead," I said. "I'm listening."

"Good." He nodded. "Want to make five grand?" He watched me.

I scratched my chin. "Legal?"

"Sure, it's all legal," he said. He pulled out a wallet and handed me a new business card. "Greg Newell, Bounty Hunter and Skip Tracer," the card read. There were license numbers on the card, indicating he was registered with the state of Idaho. I didn't know if going after people, bail jumpers and skips, even required a license in Idaho. He probably just put some numbers down to make it look official. "I had these cards made up."

"I thought you sold insurance," I said. I sipped my beer.

"I do. I also have an Amway distributorship. But this bounty hunting thing, that's where you make money." He nodded.

I looked at the card again. "How do you pronounce your last name?" I asked, kidding with him.

"It rhymes with *jewel*," he said. "Like what I got two of."

"Also rhymes with *fool*."

"You got it," he said.

"So what's this about five grand?" I asked.

"There's a guy downtown right now, he's wanted by the U.S. Marshals." He pulled out a small post office wanted poster, the tear-off kind, half size, printed on thick, white card stock. He handed the poster to me. I looked at it. The wanted man's name was Ed Holt.

"How do you know it's him?" I asked. I finished my beer and set the empty on the carpet.

"I saw him. I'm trained to be observant. He's Edward Howard Holt. I recognized him from the picture." He pointed at the wanted poster in my hand.

I looked at the poster again and read what Ed Holt was wanted for. He'd shot some cops during a Providence, Rhode Island, bank robbery years back. A couple years ago, he'd shot three more cops in Chicago when somebody recognized him and tried to arrest him. I looked at his picture. He was a short, muscular white guy, with a crew cut and a flat face. The poster said there was a twenty-five-thousand-dollar reward for his capture. "What do you want me to do?" I asked.

"I want you to help me take him in," Greg said. "We've got to deliver him to the U.S. Marshals' office in Spokane." He paused, then continued. "I need a partner on this one." He lifted his vest slightly to show me he had a pistol holstered at his waist. "In case things get touchy."

Five thousand dollars equaled a lot of stops at the package store, if it turned out to be Ed Holt. I stood. "So what do we do, partner?"

Greg stood and stuck out his right hand and we shook. He went out to his ugly truck and came back in with his Beretta. He set it on the coffee table. "Strap that on yourself someplace where you can get to it fast," he said. "He's no Girl Scout. I've got a decent crowbar in the front seat, but you can really hurt your hand smacking somebody around with that thing. Better to wing 'em and let 'em bleed a little."

I checked the safety on the Beretta, then laced up my boots and put my folding knife in the right pocket of my jeans and a pack of cigarettes in my shirt pocket. "Let's go," I said. We climbed into Greg's truck and the tires kicked rocks pulling onto the highway, headed right for town.

"Okay," Greg said, as we rode toward Main Street. "Benny owns the place, the diner. He and his family came from Mexico years ago, and I've known them for a long time. His son knows we're coming, I called him." We ran out of farm fields, and now houses passed by on the side of the road. "Anyway, if you're ever short cash, you can go in and have breakfast free. Benny's son will trust you for it as long as he knows you're working."

I nodded. It was a handy bit of information to have. "Thanks," I said.

"No problem," Greg answered. We were in town. He

turned down a side street and pulled into a parking lot. A couple of pickup trucks and a few cars sat in the sun. We saw the rear entrance to the diner. Greg got out of the truck and so did I.

"I'm going in the front," Greg said. "Stand back here and count to ten, then go in. He's sitting along the wall, facing the main street, and he's got a red ball cap on." Greg checked his pistol. "You sit in front of him, I'll sit next to him. Then we'll get him out the back door and into the truck."

"Okay," I said.

We crossed the parking lot and Greg walked around the corner. I stood next to the back door of the diner and counted to ten. Then I pushed the door open and went in. Right away I saw the man he was talking about. The place smelled like good food. Colorful paintings hung on the dull walls and the sunlight came in bright through the full-length front glass wall from Main Street. A Mexican—Benny's son, I figured—gave me a nod from the corner of the kitchen by the grill. Greg walked in the front door, walked right down the aisle, and sat down next to the man in the red ball cap. I walked up the aisle from the back of the diner and sat across from both of them. The man stopped eating his eggs and looked up.

"Who the hell are you?" the man we thought was Ed Holt said to Greg. He lifted his cup and drank a mouthful of brown coffee.

"Greg Newell," Greg said. "I'm a bounty hunter and this is my partner, John Thorn. And you're Ed Holt. We're taking you up to Spokane to the marshals'."

The man we thought was Ed Holt started to laugh. "I don't know what you're talking about," he said, chuckling. He shook his head. "My name's Bill Glass, you've got me

confused with someone else." He stared, smiling, at Greg. Then he drank some coffee.

"No, I don't," Greg said. "You're Ed Holt." Greg pulled the wanted poster out of his vest. He looked at it and looked at the man who called himself Bill Glass. Then he handed the poster over to me. I looked at it, and looked at Bill Glass. He looked like he might be Ed Holt, but I couldn't be sure. The hair wasn't right. I handed the poster back to Greg.

The man calling himself Bill Glass started to slide on the vinyl seat, as if he were going to get out of the booth. He motioned at Greg to move. "Come on, move it," he said. "I'm leaving." He had a tattoo of a parrot on his right arm.

Greg turned quickly to check Mexican Benny working in the kitchen, then shifted around in his seat to face Glass-Holt. "The only place you're going is out that back door and into my truck." He glanced at the back door and then at the man next to him. The silence was hot. Pots and pans clanged in the kitchen.

"You're crazy," said the man we suspected of being Ed Holt.

"That's right," said Greg. "I'm nuts. But I don't see you yelling for the cops to get me off you, either."

"That's because I'm Bill Glass, I live right up the road, and we take care of our own problems out here." The man who referred to himself at Bill Glass tightened his jaw. "Let's go out back together and see what all this dick-assin' around is about."

"Sure," Greg said. He slid off the vinyl booth seat and stood, waiting.

"When I get you outside," the angry man who was calling himself Bill Glass said, "I'm going to run your teeth with a stainless steel pistol. "It makes little holes going in, big holes coming out, and all I asked you to do was ride with Speedy."

I was trapped. We got up and I walked outside with the trucker who was hauling logs. I got in the passenger's side of the sleeper King Cab. It was an older rig. Speedy cranked it through the gears and we headed out of the parking lot.

"That George, he's a son-of-a-bitch, ain't he?" Speedy said.

I didn't say anything.

We curved through the mountain roads and in the side mirror I could see Beck and Carl and the others behind us. Speedy pulled over at a small cabin-unit motel. The big engine kept rolling as he put the brakes on.

"Lucky number seven," Speedy said. "Give Shipman a good talking-to."

I got out of the rig. George Beck and Carl Larson were sitting on the road in their trucks. I decided to try one last attempt at getting the hell out.

"I don't even have a gun," I said.

Speedy shrugged. "There's a pistol under the seat, take it if you need it," he said.

I reached under the seat and came out with a nine-millimeter and snapped the trigger twice at Speedy before the weight of the gun told my hand it wasn't loaded. He blinked hard, then relaxed. He smiled. It was the gun Beck had tried to hand me that night at Carl's house. I had screwed myself even tighter.

I got down out of the rig and I knew the security cameras were catching me doing it, walking with a pistol into room number seven. The door was open—I pushed it with my

along the curb." He slid off the vinyl booth seat and stood
in front of Greg. He was a little shorter than Greg but had
arms the same size. He looked mean and solid. Greg looked
soft next to him.

Greg nodded. "Sure. You give it a go," he said.

The diner patron who called himself Bill Glass reached
into his pocket and pulled out a five-dollar bill. He put it on
the table and then walked toward the back door. Greg and I
followed. The diner patron who called himself Bill Glass
nodded to Mexican Benny in the kitchen and went out
through the back door. He started to walk across the parking
lot, heading for a dark blue pickup.

"Hey," Greg called to him. "What about my teeth and
the curb?" The man who called himself Bill Glass got into a
blue pickup truck he apparently owned or at least drove and
started the engine.

Greg ran after him. The truck started to move forward
and Greg shot the front driver's side tire, practically blew
the rim off with his big Magnum revolver. Now the truck
was running on the rim, and Greg blew out the back driver's
side tire. The pickup slammed into a parked station wagon.

"For Christ's sake, help me," Greg said to me. I grabbed
the crowbar off the front seat of Greg's Toyota and followed.
Bill Glass was getting out of the truck. I swung the crowbar
for all I was worth, right into his shin. It hurt my hand, but
he went down, grabbing his leg. I yarned on it again, hard
as I could. I'd never hit anything so hard in my life. Greg
was there, flipping the injured man who had referred to himself as Bill Glass over and putting a pair of cuffs on him, so
both hands were locked behind his back. Greg grabbed the
cuffs and used them to pull the injured man to his feet. His

right leg, the one I hit, rested at an odd angle. I must have shattered it. The man was moaning with the pain and we stumbled him across the parking lot and tossed him in the back of the Toyota. Greg climbed in behind the wheel and I jumped in at copilot. I'd brought a bottle of whiskey with me, just in case, and used this moment to take a swig. I offered the bottle to Greg.

He shook his head. "You drink a lot," he said.

"I'm no fun sober," I said. I took another swig from the bottle and put it on the floor of the truck.

The man we were pretty sure was Ed Holt sat up in the backseat.

"Fucking scumbags," he screamed through the Plexiglas. He slammed against the door, but I knew Greg had engaged the childproof locks. He wasn't going anywhere. "I'll sue the shit out of both of you. My name's Bill Glass, you've got the wrong man." Then he moaned again.

We drove north in silence. Fields of grain and lentils spread out from the road on either side, an inland sea that waved with the breeze. The drive took a little over an hour and a half. We started to see the outskirts of Spokane, coming upon the Hangman Golf Course. Just after we passed the sign, the man in the back spoke. Maybe the name prompted him.

"I'm Ed Holt," Ed Holt admitted. "Why don't you boys just shoot me here and leave me?"

"Reward money," Greg answered. He eased off the accelerator. We were almost there.

Spokane is the city that time forgot. As we drove in, I read the old advertisements on the walls of the brick buildings. LION OVERALLS, THE KING OVER-ALL, A FREE PAIR IF

THEY TEAR. HENRY STRONG, A GOOD CIGAR, FOR A NICKEL. DRINK NEHI. We passed under a set of train tracks and Greg maneuvered through downtown until we were in front of the marshals' office. He left the truck running while he went inside. In a minute, he came back out with four U.S. marshals, all in plain clothes. They took the man out of the backseat of the truck and led him inside. He dragged his hurt leg. Greg followed them in, then came back out. He hopped in the driver's seat and we started back south to Moscow, Idaho. On the way home, he told me that the marshals gave him a check for the reward and he'd go to the bank with me on Monday, to settle up. We watched the fields roll by again. We talked about being partners, and how well the capture had gone. We were partners, and we'd have to do it again. Soon. Fugitive life in the West was no longer the cakewalk it had once been. Newell and Thorn were on the job. Let all the hardened criminals take notice. Somewhere on the ride home, I finished my whiskey.

Sunday came and I decided to eat breakfast at Benny's. I sat at the counter, facing the wall. Some other people were eating, but the place wasn't crowded. An older Mexican man in a white apron moved slowly down the counter and sat next to me, on the stool to my left.

"How is your breakfast?" he asked. He spoke with a thick Spanish accent.

I was eating a western omelet. "Good," I said with my mouth full.

"That's good." He smiled. His teeth were bright white. He kept on. "You're Greg's partner, right? He came in yesterday late and told me you were his partner. That you and he would hunt men together."

"Yeah," I answered. "We're partners."

"In hunting men, you are partners?"

I nodded. "Yeah, yes, I mean, in hunting men. We're partners."

We sat at the counter. A picture of a Mexican woman in a very colorful dress hung on the wall behind the counter. She was dancing. The old man looked at the picture as he spoke.

"When I first came to this country, I was one of those hunted men. One of those men who never had a chance to start over. In Mexico, they call them *los de abajo*. I think the best translation I've ever heard is 'the underdogs.' You hunt the underdogs."

Even though there were other people in the diner laughing and talking and eating, all I could hear was the old Mexican man. He kept on. "I am Benny and this is my place. For today, eat your food, finish what you have, enjoy your meal. Do not pay for this meal, since I have talked to you so much, you are my guest." He turned to look at me. "But from now on, you always pay. I know sometimes my son, he trusts. He trusts Greg when he has no money, because he knows Greg works, and now he will probably trust you, because you work with Greg." The old man shook his head. "Well, this is Benny talking. You hunt the underdogs and that is your business. But no more trust. Hunting men is not working, in my eyes." He got up from the stool and walked slowly toward the kitchen. He stopped and talked quietly with his son sweating behind the grill, and I heard the old man's words. No more trust.

Vigilance

This is what happened, the same story I gave to the investigators:

I never met Carl Larson before I rented a one-bedroom house from him in Potlatch, Idaho. I'd seen a handwritten ad tacked to a bulletin board at the University of Idaho and I called the local number from a pay phone. An old woman answered and said she and her husband were Carl's neighbors, just handled the keys for him. She'd be glad to show me the place, but I'd have to talk to Carl about renting it.

Her name was Rose. She gave me a long-distance number to reach Carl. I dialed.

A woman answered and I asked for Carl Larson and she asked what it was about. The rental, I said. A man got on the line and introduced himself as Carl Larson. He didn't mention a lease or paperwork. Nothing for me to sign. He asked me my name. Ed Snider, I lied. The utilities—phone and electric—stayed in his name. The phone was restricted from long-distance access to prevent renters from running it up, and the bill went directly to him. Same with the electric bill. All I had to do was mail him the first month's rent, a five-hundred-dollar money order made out to cash. There was a garage I could use however I wanted and Rose and her husband, Dan, would explain that to me. The house heated with a woodstove in the living room and a pellet stove in the basement. The garage woodstove worked and the neighbors would show me about turning the water on, which valve was the pressure tank, and how to empty the tank, in case I went away during a temperature drop. Keep a close eye on the pipes in winter, Carl said.

The number I'd called was in the nine-oh-seven area code, Alaska, and the mailing address he gave me was Fairbanks. Everything was to be sent care of L. Matthews, and he told me on the phone the address was the house of a woman he knew, a shirttail relation of his. He spent as little time in town as possible. He'd built a cabin way out in the woods, far away, where he hunted and fished a good part of the year. His friends on the peninsula were all big fishermen, some commercial. His voice was deep and old, a little slow in coming. We drifted into a brief conversation about states with a single area code being the best for hunting and fishing. Montana,

Idaho, and Alaska we ranked as the top three. Vermont, New Hampshire, and Maine in the East. Neither of us had traveled east in years. Carl said he liked the people out west better and I agreed. One time, he said, years and years ago, he shot a twelve-point whitetail in eastern New Hampshire, on the Maine border. He hadn't expected to see a buck that size, ever, and his rifle was undercaliber, the shot a hair too long. The hit was a solid lung shot, but the deer took off. Managed to get over the state line, marked in the woods. Carl came to a clearing and a logging road. Three Maine game wardens had the buck halfway dressed in the back of a pickup truck. Too bad about your New Hampshire deer, the one game cop said, he decided to die in Maine. That's people from the East, Carl finished.

Like he'd said, his neighbors Dan and Rose held the keys and they'd explain the trash to me, answer any questions at all. He asked me not to move stuff around in the house and to be careful with the taxidermy and I said I wouldn't and I said I would. How long did I think I'd stay in Potlatch, he asked, and I said I didn't know. I understand, he said, don't worry about it. Go look the place over and let the neighbors look you over. In the meantime, I'd mail the money order, and once it got to Fairbanks, I could move in, unless Dan and Rose didn't like the way I dressed out. He told me if I had trouble with money to ask Dan, there was always extra work around. He wished me good luck and I said the same to him. We hung up and I walked across downtown Moscow, to the post office a block off Main Street, to mail the money order. I wrote "Cash" on the To line, "Snider" on the From line.

My brother and I had given up a scrap business in Nevada,

so I carried a little money, but not much. Thirty-five hundred dollars and a truck that ran most of the time. My brother headed to Seattle after a girl, and in Seattle there were lots of girls in case he broke up with this one, so after a while you didn't even ask last names, because that wasn't important, you knew they would not be around long enough to worry about last names. Living in Potlatch put me close enough to two big colleges, Washington State and University of Idaho, both twenty minutes south. Plenty of dates if I wanted them. But I wasn't looking for that right now. I wanted to earn honest money and get on the right track. I wanted that a lot.

The one-bedroom house in Potlatch was fine. It sat fifty yards off the main road. Dan and Rose were an older couple who lived next door in a trailer with a redwood porch, and he showed me around the place. He wore a bright flannel shirt and a wide-brimmed Australian cowboy hat. He must have thought I was okay, because he let me keep the keys.

"You send the rent to Carl?" he asked.

"Yes," I said. "An hour after I talked to him."

We stood on the porch of the house. The one-bay garage was a concrete-block building next to the road. I had told Dan I hoped to fix some chain saws out of it, sharpen and sell chains to loggers.

"Do you need extra work?" he asked.

"Yes," I said. "Always."

"I can give you some work, but it's a little out of season, know what I mean? Still good work, though. Easy." He watched me.

"I shoot 'em when I see 'em," I said. "I worry about the regulations after. I've been known to keep one or two I shouldn't have. They taste the same."

Dan smiled. "You bet they do." He pointed at the garage. "See the pump behind the garage?"

I nodded. "It looks like an old gas pump."

"I'll give you the key for it. There's about ten or fifteen guys who come around and get gas from us, a dollar a gallon cash, we only sell one grade, unleaded regular, and we don't advertise."

"Where do you get the gas from?" I asked.

"A couple years ago, some big wheel from one of the universities' administration saw all the maintenance trucks pulling in and out of the gas station where both schools had their accounts. Apparently some of the boys were buying a lot of beer too, on the school card that was issued with each truck and they were looking at the girls—the point is they weren't working. Washington State is the biggest school west of the Mississippi, so that's a lot of gas and beer."

"That must have caused a problem."

"Oh, it did," Dan said. "The two schools got together and solved it by buying a mini-tanker, just five hundred gallons. And the schools bought their own big stationary tank and pump service, just to fill the mini-tanker."

"I can see where you're headed," I said.

"There are over a hundred trucks and vehicles that take gas in that fleet, not to mention lawn equipment, straight gas for the cans of mixed fuel, every single thing comes out of that mini-tank and they don't track it. They just pay the bill on the big tank and since it's less than the card system they were using, they're saving money."

"So the mini-tanker comes here once in a while?"

"Old friend of Carl's ended up with the job and as long as he's behind the wheel, we're golden. That's tax-free retirement, right there."

"How does the money work?"

"Never raise the price on the boys, it's always a dollar a gallon. Never take on any new customers, I don't care if it's your aunt Mabel. Let her get gas in town. Push the gas a little, if you've had a slow week, sell a couple cans to some loggers, just say somebody dropped it off or something. But every Friday, there should be an envelope on my porch with three hundred seventy-five dollars in it. Nothing bigger than a twenty, never take anything over a twenty and the boys know that."

"What about the driver?"

Dan smiled. "A couple years ago, he got himself into quite a fix with a woman and that woman's husband and Carl and some of Carl's friends sorted that out, so he's paying back, we're not paying him." He thought for a minute. "You know George Beck, the big fellow?"

"No," I said.

"You'll meet him, maybe. Anyway, he fixed it."

"And the rest of the money is mine?"

"Call it salary," Dan said.

"That sounds good to me," I said.

Dan patted the top porch rail. "Then welcome home," he said. "As far as I'm concerned." He walked across the gravel back to his place and Rose waved to me through the window.

I turned the garage into a fix-it shop. It had the one-car bay, three stools, and a room in the back with a cot. Lots of tools and the woodstove on one side. I sharpened chains and sold new ones for the loggers and fixed their saws. Sold bar and chain oil. The garage air compressor worked and guys were always stopping by for air in their tires. The business brought in enough to pay the rent and the one twenty-five I kept from the gas business felt good in my pocket. I listened to the loggers talk, about Montana fires and wealthy landowners who had set up their own fire stations and association. A sort of committee on wildfire vigilance. But the summer fires burned regardless and having spotters in homemade watchtowers didn't help.

At night I slept in the house and looked at the stuffed heads on the walls. Carl's small house was filled with antlers and wall mounts. A ratty looking brown horse and a burro were penned in the field next door and behind. Sometimes a sleek black horse came out and ran through the field. I fed them apples. Dan and Rose were friendly. A warm apple pie sat on my porch two days after I moved in. I watched their lights go on and off in the night. If I got up early enough, I could listen to one of them snore through the thin trailer walls. I sent Carl's mail to Alaska for him, what little there was of it, and made sure the envelope was on Dan's porch every Friday.

She pulled in one Friday evening, right next to the garage. She had a tan cowboy hat pushed back on her bright blond hair. "Put this in the garage," she said. "Close the door. I'm Carl's sister Penny from Lewiston." She paused. "Is Carl here?"

"No," I said. "He's in Alaska."

"Lucky you." She winked at me. "He doesn't do me a damn bit of good in Alaska."

Her tits swayed in her denim shirt just a little as she shut the car door. Tight jeans with a big silver cowboy belt buckle that showed off her small waist. She was gas on the fire. She walked down the driveway, into the house, and I watched her the whole way and she knew it.

I put the car in the garage, turned the lights off, and made sure the place was locked. I went into the house.

"What's going on?" I asked.

Penny sat on the couch in the front room and took the cowboy hat off. "My boyfriend's after me," she said. "Boyfriend" didn't sound right, coming from her. She was a woman, not a girl, probably in her late thirties. "I'm staying here tonight."

"Okay," I said. "Do you want to go to Moscow for pizza? I was just going."

"You get it," she said. "I'm staying here."

On the drive to Moscow, I thought about my chances of going to bed with her and decided that they weren't good and that it might screw stuff with Carl. The whole arrangement, the rental with no paperwork, the gas business, the garage. I couldn't let that slip away for big tits and a hot ass. I got to the pizza place and ordered and watched the college girls while I waited. Penny ranked right up there. I put the pizza on the front seat and drove back.

When I got there, a big guy I didn't know was sitting on the front porch smoking a cigarette. He threw it into the gravel and stood up. I guessed he was six seven or more, close to three hundred pounds. The type of man you have to shoot twice. I figured it was Penny's boyfriend and this could get mean in a hurry.

"I'm George Beck," he said, "good friend of Carl's."

We shook hands. I said, "What can I do for you?"

"You must be Ed Snider."

"That's right."

"You going to be here tonight?" he said.

"Yeah."

"Good. Penny's staying here until we can get a handle on her boyfriend."

"What's his name?" I asked.

"Tim Shipman," he said. "You don't know him, do you? We all call him Ships."

"No, I don't know him," I said. "What makes you think he'll come here?"

"You've seen Penny," he said. "If you thought she was here, wouldn't you drive up here from Lewiston?"

"Sure," I said. "I'd have already been here."

"You can see I came right away," he said, "and Penny and I broke up years ago. She'll look at you and fuck up your brain." He reached inside his coat and brought out a pistol, nine-millimeter, and tried to hand it to me. "Here," he said. "Ships is violent. This is in case he needs convincing." He held the piece out to me, butt first.

I wouldn't touch the gun. "I'll be here," I said. "And that's all that's necessary." Never touch another man's gun, because you never know what its bullets have hit. I was trying to get out of the habit of handling guns.

George slipped the pistol back inside his coat. "Suit yourself," he said, "but Ships will be strapped, so I'm just telling you." He scratched his head. Something about this wasn't quite going as planned for him.

"I'll be here," I repeated.

"Carl will appreciate that," George said. "I mean, the other thing you ought to know about Penny is that she probably did cheat on Ships or rip him off or whatever."

"I'll keep an eye out." I noticed that some makeup stained the shoulder of his jacket.

"Good," George said. "We've got some buddies in Lewiston and around and we'll take care of this." I stood looking at the ground and George went on. "Wouldn't have happened if Carl hadn't gone to Alaska." I wanted to ask why but didn't. "I'm the guy around here that gets shit done," he said. He took off and I went inside the house.

That night Penny stayed with me at Carl's place. As soon as George left and we ate the pizza, she wanted the lights off. We sat in the dark on the couch. There were only the cars passing on the main road. The lights reflected off the marble eyes of the stuffed animals. We sat there for two hours without saying a word. I watched the back field. The moon shone bright and full. The black horse was running around for some reason, but I couldn't tell which was the horse and which was the shadow. They both looked alive. Penny dozed off and I watched her small breathing, her lips and perfect nose.

Then a car pulled off the road. The door slammed and I heard footsteps over to the garage and then up to the door. The handle jiggled.

"Carl?" a man's voice asked the night. "Carl, it's me, Ships. Is Penny here?" There was a pause. "Penny?"

She was up now. She pulled me close and put her mouth

on my ear. "Pretend you're Carl," she whispered. "Use a deep voice, he won't know." Her hand was on my thigh.

I tried to use the voice I'd heard on the phone. "What?" I said in Carl's voice. "Who is it?"

"Carl," the voice said, relieved. "Carl, look, is Penny here?"

Now I was Carl. "What the hell's going on, Ships?"

"She owes me a lot of money," he said, "and she's going all around town talking."

"Talking about what?" I asked.

"About stuff she shouldn't be, is what, about you and me and George Beck and she needs to shut her mouth." He cleared his throat. "I didn't have anything to do with you guys, you know that, and she's all over town with it. She's loud wrong, is what she is."

I knew that I had been right not to touch that gun Beck had offered me. "Where is she now?" I asked.

"I thought she was here," he said. "Open the door, will you?"

"Ships, I'm busy," I said.

"If she's here, you better talk to her," he said. "And if not, I'm going to find her. She knows the whole story, I don't know why she's lying, unless she's just scared of George." He crunched gravel back to the car. The car sat there for a minute and then started again and spun out on the road.

I turned to talk to Penny, but she was already unbuttoning her shirt, standing up and pulling off her jeans. The plan I'd been following vanished and we barely made it to the bedroom. She straddled me and her whole body was smooth and tight.

*   *   *

The sex was fast and terrible. We sort of mutually stopped after a while. Just lay there. She was already pregnant, she said, which is the best birth control there is. She said it was why she was so horny. But both of us had other things on our minds. It really hadn't been worth it.

She sat on the edge of the bed, brushing her hair. "All this trouble is because Tim gave me a watch. That watch creeped me out. It was a present because I was always late. It was a man's watch, okay, but it was weird because every time I looked at it, it showed the same time. Twenty to six. It wasn't that the watch had stopped or anything, it just happened to be twenty to six when I looked at it."

She was fixing her makeup now. "Well, one month I came up short and pawned the watch. Tim and I were broken up, so what did I care? I had to write my address on the pawn slip and I bet it was a week later and two detectives and an officer came to my apartment about that watch. It belonged to an old man named Elmer Cooley from way up in the Panhandle. He'd been missing for about a month and they wanted to know how I got that watch. Cooley, they told me, had a grandson in prison who was head of a group of militiamen that live in the mountains and did I know a George Beck, they wanted to talk to him about a murder and where was my brother? So I told them the watch came from Tim Shipman and I didn't know anything else."

I had just half-fucked a woman who was involved in a possible murder, who was lying to me and lying to the cops and being actively questioned by them. She stood up to put her jeans on and I couldn't believe her body was that good, but now the whole thing was gone south. "I'd try not to worry about it," I said. "Bad coincidence." I was enough of a liar to know when I was being lied to. I'd leave at the first possible chance.

"It's on my mind all the time," she said. "What do you think Tim did?"

"I have no idea," I said. The room was much darker than the moonlit field.

"I tell people I'm married so they won't hit on me," she said.

"Does it work?" I asked. I shifted around to lean on my elbow.

"No," she said. She paused. "Men used to sit around and talk about me when I was gone. I used to be beautiful."

"You still are," I said.

"George Beck was the only man who could keep them off." She looked out to the black field. "I just didn't like some of the things he did."

It popped in my head that George Beck had been involved somehow in the disappearance of the guy named Cooley and that was what the cops were after. The watch probably came from him, not Shipman, who was trying to save his own hide.

"I'm going back to Lewiston," she said. "Tell George that's where I am and don't tell him we screwed."

"There's not much to tell," I said.

"I know," she said. "It just didn't click. We'll have to try again. I'd like to." She showed me a fake smile. "We just have to make sure George doesn't find out."

I knew she'd tell him the instant she saw him. I had half-fucked myself into a real problem. "Sure," I said. "Keep George in the dark."

"You bet," she said. "Count on it. Trust me."

When I woke in the morning, she was gone.

*   *   *

The next day I met Carl Larson. There was a knock and the door opened. I was sitting on the couch, having coffee, thinking about leaving.

"Hey," the man said. "I'm Carl. You must be Ed."

"That's right, that's right," I said. "I didn't expect you back."

"There were some problems." He waved his hand.

"That's too bad," I said.

"Is that your truck by the garage, the black one?"

"Yes," I said.

"How did that happen?" he said.

"What?" I asked.

"I think you've got four flat tires," he said.

I stepped onto the porch. My truck sat lopsided by the garage and the rims rested right on the ground. I wouldn't be running anywhere too soon. I went back in.

Carl walked around the place. I suppose he wanted to see if I'd moved anything. I hadn't. Then he came out to the living room and sat in the chair by the door.

"George Beck called me and said my sister Penny was in trouble."

"That's right," I said.

"How come you didn't call me? Or write?"

I shrugged. "It wasn't my place to do that, George said he was taking care of it. It only came about the other day."

Carl shook his head. "Don't do that again," he said. "If my sister comes to you for something, let me know right away."

"Okay," I said. "From now on I will."

"Thank you," he said.

"I didn't even know you had a sister."

"No offense taken," he said. "Now I'm going down to Lewiston to visit her and see if I can straighten this out."

"Okay."

"I should be back in a couple days and we'll work out some sort of arrangement when I get back."

"The garage is fine for me," I said. "As long as I can cut my rent in half."

"Go ahead," Carl said. "While I'm here sleeping in the house, just pay half. That should give you about a month at half rent."

"Fine," I agreed. "I'll pay it now, cash." I pulled a roll of bills out of my front pocket and counted two hundred fifty dollars in front of him and handed it to him.

"See you in a couple days."

As soon as he was gone down the road, I went out to patch my tires. It was no use. They'd never hold air again. Someone had taken a jagged blade and ripped each tire completely around the sidewall. Whoever it was had to have been a very big, strong man.

The next day the phone rang and I let the machine answer and it was Carl from Lewiston.

"Pick up," he said. "It's Carl."

I picked up the phone and he went on. "Is my sister there?"

"No," I said.

"Did you fuck her?" he said.

"No," I said. It sounded wrong.

"George Beck says you did. We'll talk about that when I get back. Go check the mail for me."

Sure enough, there was a letter from Penny. The postmark showed Portland, Oregon, and I told him that. He asked me to read it to him over the phone. And I did. It was a story about Tim Shipman, but completely different than the one she had told me. She'd been telling everyone that Tim Shipman might have murdered someone. She was doing that, she said in the letter, because George Beck had given her that watch and she knew damn well what was going on. George Beck was killing people in some rival gang, George Beck was moving speed. George Beck killed some old man Cooley in the woods near the Columbia River. George Beck had better pay her for keeping his name out of it, but if the cops caught Ships, he'd spill the whole thing. Ships knew about the watch and George Beck and Elmer Cooley.

"That's it?" Carl asked.

"Yes," I said.

"I'll be back in a while," he said. "Sit tight." He hung up.

An hour later, George Beck showed up. Two other guys pulled in, too. My truck just sat there, completely useless to me on flat tires. Mac, one of the gas customers, also pulled in with his rig. He eyed George Beck.

"Just come back tomorrow," I said. "I'll take care of you then, if you can wait."

He lowered his voice. "Never certain if tomorrow's going to show, with people like that around," he said. "You take care and I'll see you when you don't have company." He pulled back onto the road.

"Why don't you close up now?" George Beck said. "You're going with us."

"I don't think so," I said. "Carl didn't say anything about this."

"You can go with us," he said, "or never go anywhere again."

"Fine," I said.

We drove to a truck stop in Montana, seven miles over the Idaho border. George Beck and his two buddies sat in a booth drinking coffee and ordered food and Carl showed up and we sat there eating.

George waved to a trucker at the counter. "That's Speedy," he said. "You ride in his rig and we'll be behind you."

"Where are we going?" I asked.

"We're going to talk to Tim Shipman and straighten this out. He's hiding in a motel over here, but we found him."

"What's Speedy got to do with it?"

George Beck got bigger in the booth. "I don't know, you see, because I'm dumb," he said. "People expect me to do dumb things. For instance, you fucked Penny and I'm so dumb I just found out about it, just now, this instant. So we can all drag you out in the parking lot and in the middle of things, a gun goes off and dumb local boy George Beck shot the man who was fucking his woman behind his back and the jury comes in, local folks, and they see me, and they know what I'm about and who I'm friends with, and I go do two years. You think two years is going to bother me? I'll come out of prison with more friends than I've got now." He pulled his coat back a little to show me a shoulder holster

foot—and saw Shipman on the bed, the side of his head gone from gunshot wounds. He'd been shot less than an hour earlier. I sat on the edge of the bed for a minute, trying to draw them into the room, or within camera range. Don't throw up, I told myself, you always throw up. But nobody came, and eventually I just walked out. Speedy was gone. George Beck and Carl Larson had pulled down the road a ways. I walked and got in the back of Carl's truck and we rode all the way to Potlatch. This time I kept the gun.

After that George moved in with Penny and they were considered married by everybody. Shipman's body was found in a Dumpster ten miles from the motel, but the paper said the cops knew the body had been moved. Then I heard George Beck was being held in Boise on a federal warrant and was also wanted by the Mounties in Lethbridge on a gun charge and possible murder of a witness in a homicide case in Washington State. This just made me anxious. Penny had the baby, a girl, late the following spring. Soon there was another man living there with her, and I tried not to think about it.

Carl went back to Alaska and nobody really came to the shop after that, except the gas customers. I was in Moscow picking up a case of oil one day and saw Mac, the old logger, in the parking lot. He was talking to some men. He nodded at me.

"I could use some work," I said. "Maybe you could get me a job as a fire spotter. With the park service or private. Like you talked about that one time, that private association of landowners in Montana."

"No," he answered. "No thanks. The woods are all full.

It'll burn with or without you. You should ask George Beck
for work, he probably needs somebody to clean his cell or
something."

I came back to the garage and Dan must have seen me pull
in, because he came out of his trailer and over to the garage.

"Some men stopped by here looking for you. Knocked on
my door. Frightened Rose." He handed me a business card.
It was from an attorney in Spokane.

"What's this?"

"What is it?" he said. "It's fucking yours, that's what it is,
but it ended up on my doorstep, how is that?" He didn't
raise his voice, but he was clear. "Just because I don't believe
in heaven and angels doesn't mean I don't believe in hell and
demons. You need to get that shit straight in your head.
Realize what you're involved in. Separate the concepts." He
pointed at his trailer. "I've got a purpose here on Earth,
which is to provide for and protect Rose. You seem to be
about to sign on as a short-order man in the devil's butcher
shop. You're on a bad path, with bad men. Those two things
put us at odds. There might be a time when someone with a
badge comes around asking questions about you and George
Beck and Carl."

"And you'd rat?"

He shook his head. "Never. It's not the law that concerns
me, not a single bit. I want to make sure you and I have an
understanding. The law doesn't stop a thing. Consequences
only come after and after is too late, far as I'm concerned."
He pointed at the pen behind his house. "My brother's
bringing me up a good dog from his farm and everything in

my place is loaded with the safety off. Whoever buys the ticket will get an express trip if I can help it and I'm here to tell you, although she was a lot of trouble different times, I love my Rose and I love my job of protecting her. Knock on my door and I'll let Remington answer it. Both barrels."

"I understand," I said.

"See that you do," Dan said. "Or there will be pieces of you they'll never find." He started to walk back to his trailer. "We're not all hicks and cousin-fuckers up here," he said over his shoulder. "Do your business somewhere else. You mistook kind for simple," he finished. He shut the trailer door.

I called the Spokane lawyer from a pay phone and once I got past the secretary the first thing he asked me was did I still have that gun. Sure, I said, and it's keeping me alive. Because that's the gun that killed Elmer Cooley. Well, maybe it is and maybe it isn't, he said, and if I wanted to rely on that, put my whole life on the line for one ballistics test, then I could go right ahead. And I knew he was right, although I hoped otherwise.

The Feds were leaning on George Beck hard and he was going to inform on me, said the lawyer. His buddy at the motel had a videotape of me walking into Tim Shipman's room with a pistol and coming out and a Polaroid shot of Shipman lying dead on the bed. My name was going to be tied to all this, unless I could get Beck's lawyer some good information on the remaining members of the Cooley family who still lived in the Panhandle. The Cooleys ranked high on the Feds' most wanted list and usable information about them would loosen pressure on George Beck, would reduce his charges.

What Beck and his lawyer didn't know was that if the Feds got hold of my prints, my days as Ed Snider were over.

I wasn't going to take the rap Beck was ready to hand me. I'd get the information and be gone. I hid George Beck's nine-millimeter up underneath the dashboard of my truck, held by electrical tape to the fire wall. The truck stayed locked. That gun was the only thing that connected Beck to the murder of Elmer Cooley and I kept it for no reason other than desperation. I drove north into the Panhandle, past Priest Lake and further, headed to the Cooleys' house to do the best rat work I could.

I liked the Cooleys right off, which was tough on my brain. Over those first two winter months, I tried to adjust. It was them or me. They bought my cover without a question, just a guy up to log some adjacent land. No big deal. Pop Cooley and I ate dinner together a couple of times. One working man talking to another in the mountains. Talking about making a living in a place where that was real tough work. I liked him and I liked the kid. After sixty days, I had them on a talking basis.

The kid sat in a green plastic lawn chair in the snow behind my three-room cabin. Light was just coming. The kid propped his feet on an empty propane cylinder. He wore a dark blue jacket against the cold. Under his watch cap he had a home haircut. He was whittling a stick with the new pocketknife his father gave him for Christmas. I knew he was whittling weird little smiley faces, even though I couldn't see that far. I found the sticks everywhere, the kid did it to every piece of wood he came across. Small, crooked smiley faces and the word PEELER, his nickname. He couldn't have been more than fourteen. As soon as he heard me awake, banging and emptying ash from under the woodstove, he was at the back kitchen door. He was skinny, but tall with a man-size head.

"Well if it isn't Kid Cooley," I said, "bantamweight champion of the Pacific Northwest. How do you feel before the big fight, Kid, say something for the fans? Are you still single, the girls have been asking."

The kid half-smiled and then got serious. "No power, right, you got no power, no juice?"

I snapped the light switch back and forth. The kitchen ceiling light stayed off. "No juice," I said. I had rented the cabin from the Cooleys for two months now and the power was always steady, which is rare in the mountains and deep woods. It tends to flicker. A single light came from the Cooleys' house, further above me on the hill. "You got lights, though."

"Jap generator," the kid said. "Pop put it in a year ago, hard-wired it from out in back, so they couldn't cut power on us."

I sat on a folding chair at the card table in kitchen. "How am I going to have coffee, Kid?"

The kid pointed at the rusted set of blue, white, and black camp pots hung behind the stove on what used to be the fireplace. "Pop says you got to give us a ride today. Pop says we're the soldiers and he's the general."

His father was standing right outside the kitchen door and raised his voice from there. "I did not say that, I most certainly did not, nobody has to give us a ride anywhere, I said catch him before he left for work if he was working today and see what he said. That's what I said." He cleared his throat as he came into the kitchen. "Seems we were vandalized in the night, somebody cut the tires on the Jeep and the power's out." The Cooleys used an old Jeep with its stick on the column to get around. The back fender was rusted except for a bumper sticker. MARINE SNIPER: YOU CAN RUN, BUT YOU'LL JUST DIE TIRED. Pop had been in the Corps, with Vietnam action under his belt. He mentioned it when I first moved in and saw the sticker. Pop's father, Elmer Cooley, had been involved in the white gangs that live in the Pacific Northwest. Elmer had been murdered, he said, in the woods of Eastern Washington, near the Columbia River. Elmer was buried up the hill, in the family plot near the house. Elmer had lived in the cabin I was renting and I knew Pop kept alert.

"Did you hear anything in the night?" I asked. "Did the dog go after anything?"

"I had the dog inside with me because of those big bears coming around lately, too close to the house," Pop said. "I didn't want Cannon getting mauled."

"Sure," I said. "Where do you need to go today?"

"Spokane," he said. "To the train station."

"What's going on there?" I asked.

"My younger brother's coming home," he said. "He just got done doing ten years of federal time. He maxed out."

"That's a long time," I said.

"I don't think they could give Jack enough time to beat him," he said. "When he was a kid, eighteen really, he did five years here state time for some shit. Now he's done ten more and he won't be forty until August. You'll see when we pick him up. Jack's a stone house, inside and out. Always has been, always will be."

"Hey, Snider," the kid said. "Let me wear your bullet-proof, since we're going into the big city."

He had tried on my vest before and loved it. "Sure," I said. "I wouldn't want anybody to mess with you. Big city of Spokane, tough town." I tightened it on him, made sure he was comfortable.

We climbed in my truck, heading south through the woods and mountains, under the eyes of hawks and eagles, two hours to Spokane.

The lines were down because I'd dropped a limb on them. The tires were flat because I'd cut them. I wondered if Pop, somewhere in his mind, didn't suspect this. He wasn't a stupid man, when it came to hunting and fishing and fields of fire and decoy interest. All manner of blinds, lures, and smoke to fool the enemy. He talked hunting to Peeler as we drove. If he suspected, he never let on. He needed to get to Spokane and I was the only man available for the job. I had made myself that way, cut myself to fit. Purposefully become a piece of the puzzle. Cold sweat ran down over my ribs and bled into my T-shirt all the way to the train station. Jack Cooley wasn't a Girl Scout. He'd started out with the Hammerskins and moved up to the elite Eighty-eight Dragoons. Federal law enforcement blamed the Dragoons for a host of crimes, but most recently tied them to a shoot-out in Wyoming where five officers died raiding a meth lab and supposed Dragoon safe house. I knew any information I got out of Jack Cooley would be all George Beck needed to loosen his own state-held noose. George Beck had been in the woods of Eastern Washington the day Elmer Cooley died, and although they couldn't prove he pulled the trigger, they were applying pressure. When it comes to law enforcement, they prosecute deaths of their own kind hardest. Everybody else is just a scumbag to them anyway, or was involved in stuff that they deserved to die for. We didn't catch you at it, but you've got to be guilty of something, something you did before or something we don't know about.

The train station in Spokane is brick, a mix of new and old. Jack Cooley wasn't there yet, his train was late. The kid rode up and down on the escalators and had a soda. Pop sat on the wood benches and watched the people with their luggage, buying tickets. When I went to sit next to Pop, there on the bench was a small smiley face and PEELER written underneath. The kid went down the escalator again, back up. Then the train arrived.

Jack Cooley was one of the first ones to come out of the arrival door and start walking toward us. He was an inch taller than I was and broad in the shoulders. He wore an old army jacket and jeans and work boots. The kid went right over to him and hugged him and Jack hugged him back.

"Peeler," Jack said. "Fucking little Peeler. Jesus Christ." He hugged the kid again.

Pop went over and shook hands with Jack and hugged him with one arm. He introduced me. "This is Ed Snider, he's renting Grandpa's house while he does some contract logging over on the edge of old Freleigh's property. He drove us today."

Jack Cooley looked me up and down. "Thanks," he said. He motioned at Pop and the kid. "These are nice people to be nice to."

"Glad you're out," I said.

"You're never out after that long," Jack answered. "The cell just gets a little bigger." He looked around at the vending machines and pay phones by the door. "Come on," he said. "Let's get up in those mountains. I've been dreaming about them for ten years. Are they still there?"

"Nothing's changed," Pop said. "Nothing's changed."

The kid stopped to take a piss before we got in the truck and when he came out, he had another can of soda with him. He shook it before he got in my truck. He cracked the can open and sprayed Jack with the soda and Jack was laughing and shaking his head soaking wet. "I'll clean it," the kid said. "Pop told me we shouldn't use champagne, so I used soda."

"Peeler," Jack said, "you should never sleep too heavy." He was laughing as he said it.

I drove the Cooley family back to tip of the Idaho Panhandle. By the time we got home, it was snowing lightly and the three of them walked up the hill to their house while I reloaded my woodstove for the night.

The next morning I had been up for a while when Jack Cooley came down for a cup of coffee. He was still wearing the old army jacket.

"How're you doing?" I asked.

"Fine," he said. "Same as always."

"How was it inside?"

"Brutal," he said and left it at that.

"Where'd you do most of your time?"

He sipped his coffee. "Kentucky. Pennsylvania."

He was right across the table from me, so I had to ask. "Pop said you might come out and go after some people."

Jack shook his head. He rubbed his chin. "I'm not doing anything to anybody up here, not a thing. I'm not involved in anything other than my own life."

"Do they know that?" I asked.

He put his coffee down. "Everything with you is a question," he said. "Who is they?"

"I didn't mean anything by it," I said.

"The only people here are you and me, Pop, and Peeler. Is that right?"

"Hey," I said, "I misspoke myself."

"I'm not moving off this mountain until yesterday is dead, do you get my meaning?" he asked.

"Yes," I said.

"I'm not hiding up here," he said. "I'm out."

"I believe you," I said.

"You ever see a nest of snakes in the woods? Sometimes they'll be in a rotted tree trunk or out in a field?"

I nodded.

"Crawling all knotted up with each other, biting each other, this one eating the tail of that one that's eating the head of another, sliding all around each other, so you can't tell which one is which one. Some poor people think that's life." He reached down and brought his coffee up, took a swallow. He was looking at the mountains. He set his coffee on the table and started for the door. "Solitary never bothered me," he said. "It was being in population that I didn't care for. Too many snakes." He went out and I watched him walk back up the hill through the ankle-deep snow.

The next day I drove to Spokane alone. George Beck's lawyer met me downtown and we talked near the water, in the park.

"What did you find out?" he asked.

"Nothing. Jack Cooley isn't doing anything in any organization, as far as I can tell yet." We walked along a side street and pretended to look at the shops.

"This isn't what we agreed on, this isn't going to help George. You've got to dig around and find something."

"These people don't trust me," I said. "And they don't talk much under the best of circumstances. Jack's still wearing his prison laundry army coat, for God's sake."

"Fine," he said. "Tomorrow, George is going to begin talking about Tim Shipman and you and that Larson girl and you can deal with the fallout from that on your own." He started to walk away. "The gun won't help you. We're going forward."

"That's no good," I said. "I need more time."

"Two days," he said. "And here." He handed me a pad and pen. "Draw me a map of where the Cooleys are, so if it comes to it, the sheriffs can get a decent address for the warrant."

I drew the map as best I could and if someone was really bent on finding it, they'd find it. I handed the pad back to him.

"That will buy you two days with me, but after that, George talks and signs statements and testifies and your name is on everything."

When I got home, there was a sandwich on my kitchen table and a small stick with a smiley face on it. As I went to put wood in the stove, I realized that several of the logs carried messages. PEELER, on each one of them. PEELER.

The next morning Cannon was scratching at my door and I came out. Something was in the road, about fifty yards from my house. I thought it was Jack, facedown in the snow. I recognized the army jacket. Cannon started back toward his house and when I looked up, Pop and Jack were running down the road, toward me.

"They shot Peeler," Pop yelled to no one.

"I didn't hear a shot," I said.

"Nobody heard it," said Jack.

When we got close I could see a faint spray of blood around Peeler's head. I threw up into the snow. Not at any time had shooting the kid been discussed. Beck's people would push until something gave. Either me or Jack Cooley. I threw up again.

"Why the fuck did they shoot Peeler?" Jack asked the sky.

I realized Peeler had Jack's coat on.

"He drew the fire," Pop said. "He walked around in it the other morning, I thought maybe you had some cigarettes in there and he was trying out smoking."

When we got close, we could see Peeler was still breathing, even though there was blood coming out of his nose.

"Peeler?"

His mouth opened and his voice, scratchy and cracked, came out. "Pop," the kid groaned. "It hurts."

Jack rolled him over, pulled back the coat. He was wearing the Kevlar vest, my bulletproof. He'd been hit, twice, body shots. He was hurt, but he was alive. Jack carried him up to the house.

"What can I do?" I said.

"Keep an eye out," Pop said.

I took George Beck's pistol out of the truck, grabbed some shells Pop had given me when I first got there, and went walking. I went into the woods, to try to see if I could spot anyone.

Down the hill a ways, on the other side of the Cooleys' house, was a small family cemetery. I stopped for a minute. Pop had told me who was in there, where his family tree had branched. Outside the cemetery, I noticed a pick and a shovel. Jack must have been down there. It looked like he was getting ready to dig a new grave. Peeler had carved some sticks and one was in the shape of a cross. The stick read, GEORGE BECK, SENT TO HELL BY THE COOLEYS.

I walked back to my cabin. Somehow, while in the shadow of prison yards and guards and friends and enemies, Jack already knew who killed his grandfather.

An hour later, Pop came down to my door. "Do you think," Pop asked me, "you could go into town and get some cigarettes and coffee and groceries, could you do that?"

"Sure," I said. "I'll do it right now." It was my only way out.

I drove through town and kept going. Maybe they were planning my burial, too. For such big country, things had closed in on me rapidly. I needed to get out of rifle range of these people.

*   *   *

That fall, in one of the big shipping yards out in Grays Harbor, a guy who looked a lot like me started running a forklift and a log loader. He didn't eat with anybody, didn't talk to anybody. He cashed his check in the bar across the street and lived in a two-room apartment over the pool hall. He walked to work. The name he gave people was Tom Miller and he worked at the yard for six months. He didn't miss a day.

Monday came, time to clock in, then noon, and the foreman noticed Miller's card still in the rack. He asked around, did anybody know where Miller was? One guy said he heard Miller say he had a sister in California. He never said that to me, somebody else spoke up. Said he was from right here near Tacoma, born and raised. He didn't want to go fishing Friday, someone said. We asked him to go fishing, said we were taking our kids and he was welcome, and he said no thanks.

I guess he quit, the foreman said when Miller hadn't showed by the end of the day. So if anybody knows anybody looking for work and can run a loader and show up on time, the job pays four fifty a week, you do your own taxes as a subcontractor and don't talk union here. Sitting behind his desk in his office, the foreman cut Miller's time card in half and threw it in the garbage.

Tom Miller hadn't quit. Somebody with sharp eyes and a long memory spotted him. The man who called himself Tom Miller couldn't report to work because he was being held in a little room in the basement of a Seattle courthouse. Held until the investigators arrived.

*   *   *

After I told this whole story to the investigators, they kept me in custody for a couple of days. They told me that the man who lived with Penny Larson and her daughter was fatally shot in a hunting accident in the mountains of Northern Idaho, not far from their house, but managed to struggle into Canada before he died. The Mounties found him. They told me George Beck had been released. They told me Carl Larson was missing. They told me that Jack Cooley might be dead but that Peeler was still alive. They told me they knew I'd been Ed Snider for a while.

Then the investigators approached me about being an informant down in Oregon, on the Rogue River, where a group of white supremacists was moving meth and dogs and guns. We want you to do this, they said. Not that you have much choice. Sure, I said, I'll do it. But all I wanted was out. The whole sky seemed covered with heavy-gauge mesh steel, one big prison. If I was lucky to be alive, I rarely knew it. Normal men get to be things. Sons and husbands, fathers and friends. I was not any of those things. I tried, but this is me telling you I failed.

So I went in undercover, and in the middle, the fucking middle of it all, there was an hour when nobody was watching me and I had a little money and I slipped away, on the ghost train out of there.

I can't even imagine how many people are looking for me now.

The title "Underdogs" was inspired by Mariano Azuela's 1915 novel *Los de Abajo,* translated as *The Underdogs* in English versions. A practicing physician, Azuela is known as the Mexican Chekhov, although he's probably closer to Gorky.

Acknowledgments

I was very fortunate to have such a good team of people helping me, in various ways, with this book and they deserve both credit and thanks.

At Scribner, Colin Harrison is a great editor, a master word carpenter, a friend, and a fine novelist as well. He lives fiction and words and certainly helped me a great deal. He gave beyond time to this book and believed and supported it (and its author) in ways writers dream of.

Sarah Knight is the best assistant in the world, bar none. Absolutely fantastic.

I'm very grateful to Susan Moldow. Nan Graham went out of her way for me and I appreciate that. Caroline Murnane has been very helpful and it was terrific to work with her. Erin Cox is equally great to work with and goes above and beyond, every time, with a smile and energy. I'm lucky to be at Scribner.

At ICM, Sloan Harris is the king of agents and a great reader, a friend, and a friend to writers. He put a lot of time and effort into making this happen.

Katharine Cluverius never let me down, not once, and I really appreciate her work. I'm lucky to be at ICM.

My friends and family—thanks beyond words.

The remarkable firm of R&RM. Anthony Neil Smith, Chief Crimedog and Victoria Esposito-Shea, thank you.

A special thanks to Eric Gagne (Game over!) and Paul Lo Duca, sadly departed now, maybe to return, and the Los Angeles Dodgers. To the American Legion, old soldiers who deserve our thanks, and who provide the means for summer baseball all across the country. To the men and women in the armed services who defend our country. Love the soldier, hate the war.

Thanks to all the faculty, especially Alan Ziegler, Richard Howard, and David Plante and my classmates at Columbia. Roar, Lions, roar.

Otto Penzler is the don of crime and mystery fiction, a great editor and owner of The Mysterious Bookshop and the stories here have benefited greatly from my association with Otto and *The Best American Mystery Stories*.

Michele Slung is the most amazing reader, the reader all writers dream about. Michele deserves extra applause, always, for everything.

Other people take pictures, but Joyce Ravid sees deeper than that.

To the ATL, M-world, WSBW and best brother Will.

About the Author

SCOTT WOLVEN is a writer living in upstate New York. His stories have appeared in *The Best American Mystery Stories* (2002, 2003, 2004).

Printed in the United States
By Bookmasters